MW00944491

THE SELECTION

THE FORGOTTEN CHRONICLES BOOK ONE

Jason J. Nugent

Jason J. Nugent
jasonjnugent.com

Publisher's Note: This is a work of fiction. Names, charac-
ters, places, and incidents are a product of the author's
imagination. Locales and public names are sometimes used
for atmospheric purposes. Any resemblance to actual people,
living or dead, or to businesses, companies, events, institu-
tions, or locales is completely coincidental.

Book Layout © 2016 BookDesignTemplates.com

The Selection: The Forgotten Chronicles Book One/ Jason J.
Nugent. — 1st ed.

ISBN: 9781544244518

To my son Jackson. This story is for you.

One

Mina giggled. Eron ran across the playground. "Mina, I love you! Will you be my girl? You're so beautiful—" He tripped on a rock and face planted on the red soil. When he stood, Mina had fallen over with laughter.

"Aw, come on Mina, that's not funny!"

"Yeah it is! Look at you!" She pointed at his shirt, stained red.

"Yeah, whatever," he said.

They were on morning recess, expending boundless energy while teachers relaxed. The children were more excited than usual at the long siren blast indicating the Selection was underway.

"Ten years from now when you turn eighteen, it's gonna be your turn at the Selection," Mina said. She held out her hands with fingers splayed. "Ten!" she said.

"Yeah? So what? It's how we become men," Eron replied. He puffed out his chest and Mina giggled again.

"Don't kill anyone, though, 'cause that's bad."

Eron cocked his head. "Why would I do that?"

Mina's grin faded. "'Cause that's what you gotta do. I don't want you to, though." She approached him, her red curls bouncing with each step. "I kinda like you, too, Eron," she whispered in his ear as she kept walking. His face turned as red as the Anastasian sun. The bell rang and the children ran for the school doors.

At the afternoon recess, Mina gathered with a group of her friends, all girls. Eron considered joining the group, but so many girls together at once intimidated him. Instead, he sat by himself and watched the other students playing. There were more boys than girls in his school. After the Selection, however, he knew that would change. Afterwards there were always more adult females than males.

"Why aren't you with Mina?" a voice behind Eron called. It was Bello. He liked the larger boy, even though he tended to be mean.

"Oh, hey Bello. I don't know. She's with her friends. I don't wanna bother her."

Bello sat next to him, his large frame casting a shadow over Eron. "So what? Are you scared? Don't be a baby."

"Shut up, Bello! Just drop it, ok?"

"I heard you tell her you loved her. Oooh, you love her, don't ya, Eron?" Bello stood. "Hey Mina," he called. Mina and her friends looked over. Eron shoved his face in his hands. "Mina, did you know Eron loves you? He looooooves you!"

Mina's friends laughed.

"Be quiet, Bello! Don't say anything!" Eron said.

"Eron loves Mina! Eron loves Mina!" Bello sang. Mina's friends laughed, and others on the playground joined in.

"Come on now, stop laughing. Bello, please stop. You're embarrassing him," Mina said. Bello laughed harder.

"No, I'm not. Look," he said, pointing at Eron. Eron

shook, veins pulsing on his forehead.

"You're not embarrassed, are you?" Bello asked. Eron looked up, his eyes red and glistening. He opened his mouth to reply, then stopped.

"Seriously, Mina, he loves you!" Bello said.

Eron faced Bello, the larger boy standing a head taller than him. "Shut. Up."

"But it's the truth."

Eron clenched his fists.

"What, are you gonna hit me?"

"Eron, please. No violence. You don't need to do anything. It's ok," Mina said, her calm voice soothing to Eron.

"Yeah, you don't need to do anything," Bello said, mocking her. Eron turned and walked calmly away.

"That's it, Eron, walk away like a coward," Bello said.

Eron ignored his taunts and left the playground, Mina trailing after him.

"Hey," she said. He'd made it to the school doors and stopped.

"What?" he replied.

"Don't worry about Bello. He's just a bully. No one thinks bad about you. Promise."

"Sure, no problem."

"Eron, I do like you. Don't let him get to you."

The boy paused, then grasped the door handle and left her standing outside.

That was the last time he spoke with her during grade school. Other than an occasional smile and a hi, he couldn't muster enough courage to talk to her.

Bello's taunts continued and intensified. They were separated several times on the playground, Bello nearly beating up the smaller boy each time. Mina tried to intervene, but her actions seemed to make it worse. Whatever she said to Bello didn't help Eron.

By the time they reached high school, Eron's crush on Mina deepened.

"Why don't you just try talking to her?" his close friend Connor asked. He'd known Connor since they were little, but they didn't begin to hang out until eighth grade. As freshmen, they'd become best friends.

They sat in Eron's room playing chess.

"I can't, Connor. Not now."

"Why not? She's just a person like me. You talk to me. Why not her?"

Eron shrugged. "It's different. She's a girl and you're not." Connor sighed.

A loud siren blared.

The Selection had begun.

Eron jumped. "Timo!" he said. His older brother Timo was now eighteen, old enough for inclusion in the Selection. He'd been anxious about the event, and now the sirens called him to action.

Eron and Connor raced from the room, nearly slamming into Timo.

"Timo, it's time," Eron said. His brother looked at him with wide eyes, a blank expression on his face.

"Yeah, I guess it is. Goodbye, Eron. I'll see you when you get there."

Their mom hugged her older son. "Goodbye, son. Be safe. Do what you must. You can do this. Don't forget your knife." She kissed his cheek and he nodded.

Timo marched out the door and fell in line with the rest of the boys.

"Sorry, Connor, I gotta go," Eron said. He sprinted after his brother.

"Timo! Wait! Wait up!"

His brother didn't turn around. Eron followed as far as he could until the soldiers in gray uniforms forced him back, telling him to go home.

Two

Eron couldn't forget Timo's bloodcurdling screams. The sound pierced his eardrums, making him wince. Timo had always been a strong boy, full of adolescent bravery and confidence beyond his years, but when forced to enter the Selection, he howled and screamed.

That was the last time Eron saw his brother-before Timo's ear-splitting screams began to echo in his head. Eron often wondered what happened to him on that day two Earth years before.

Several weeks after Timo disappeared, Eron woke in the middle of the night, screaming loudly and punching the air. His mother tried to comfort him, explaining Timo had to go through this rite of passage. She assured him Timo's actions were overly dramatic. Eron know he, too, would have to eventually endure the Selection.

That's probably what bothered him the most—knowing one day he'd face the inevitable event looming in the future, unless he could stop himself from turning eighteen. Growing anxiety about the Selection had gnawed at him since Timo's experience.

School studies suffered because of it, but most teachers understood. They knew what was waiting for Eron and the other boys his age. Anastasians had instituted it centuries ago while they were yet a small colony. Still, Eron's mother didn't let that excuse stop her from berating Eron for his slipping grades.

"Eron, how many times have I told you to apply yourself? You can do better than this! Look at these grades. A D in history! History, of all things! You're better than that!"

"But, mom! I've got a lot on my mind. Don't you understand?"

"What I understand is I have a seventeen-year-old son who thinks skirting through school will help him as an adult! Your studies are the most important thing right now, son. Knowledge is everything. There's no room for incompetence. Take it seriously if you expect to make something of yourself. You're smart. Why are your grades dropping like this? A D in chemistry and an F in literature? Eron, I raised you better than this!"

Eron opened his mouth to reply, but the stern look on his mother's face silenced him. He wanted to tell her his fears about the Selection; about how much losing his brother hurt. But as she stood with her hands on her hips, staring with deep, glistening eyes, he dropped it. Excuses never went far with her.

"I'm sorry, mom. I'll try better. I am doing better right now, actually," he lied. Diffusing her was his priority, and if lying to her achieved his goal, then so be it. He hated resorting to this, but it was something he'd learned well before Timo left. Being the youngest child, Eron felt like she'd stored up all her leftover anger from his older sister and brother to take out on him.

He hadn't seen Samantha in years. The last he knew, she lived at an outpost on the far side of Anastasia. She married and had a child of her own. Eron's family didn't attend the hasty wedding and he'd never met his nephew. Since they lived so far away, he never saw them. On planet communications were restricted for military use. Hearing from her was only through letters, which they received sporadically.

Eron's mother talked little about her. Samantha was five Earth years older than Eron and she'd been gone since he was thirteen. So much had changed in her life—and in his, for that matter— since she left, that it felt much longer. He hoped to reconnect with her one day.

Eron hugged his mom. "I'm doing better, mom, I swear. You'll see on my next report card." She squeezed him tight. It was just the two of them now, and they were close. His father had been gone for many years. Eron used to have a clear picture of his father's face in his mind. Over time it faded to a vague image of a man who was fun and warm. He wouldn't have been able to pick him out of a crowd.

According to his mom, his dad left for the Anastasian Defense Force, a small but necessary militia. All males over age thirty were required to register, and there were no guarantees they'd ever return. Eron's mom talked about him on the long, lonely nights when she'd had a bit too much wine, saying, "They don't do anything," and, "He's probably on the other side, enjoying Victory Point." Other than that,, she rarely talked about him. Sometimes her denial bothered Eron. He wondered if he, too, would be someone she seldom spoke of once he left for the Selection.

She finally released Eron from her embrace and he went to his room to read. He'd been learning about television and the internet in the Earth history lessons he did so poorly on. Those luxuries weren't for most Anastasians. The military used similar technology, but those resources weren't abundant on Anastasia. The scientists and thinkers on planet hadn't yet figured out how to convert Anastasian resources to Earthlike devices and equipment. It was an unforeseen problem still not resolved. Earth stopped sending equipment because of what Eron's history book called "the Ultimate War," and since then, Anastasia was stuck in a strange technological stasis.

Not that it really mattered much, though. Eron wouldn't have had the time to watch television shows or play computer games anyway. His grades were slipping. He needed to focus now, no matter what awful things awaited him at the Selection.

All the boys in his class faced the same fate. One day, they would enter the Selection unless physically or mentally unable. Eron could remember a few of those instances over the years, however, most faced the Selection and were never seen again. Rumor had it that those who went through the process lived a wonderful life in another colony, maybe on an outpost like his sister. They'd come through the Selection stronger and more capable to help grow Anastasia's dwindling population. The projected population growth did not pan out as expected upon human arrival three hundred years before.

Boys told stories of beautiful girls awaiting the survivors of the Selection, that girls would fight over them for the honor to marry one of the brave. It was almost as if the boys needed to believe in the fantasy to accept their fate, but Eron wasn't convinced. But for Timo's sake, he hoped it was true.

Timo's screams echoed through his head again, the awful sounds of agony stabbing at his brain. When Timo set off for the Selection, he'd put on his bravest face. He told Eron not to worry; that he'd make it through, and one day when Eron went through the Selection and survived, they'd meet up and revel in their victories.

But that was before the rest of the boys were released. Then, everything changed for Eron. As he watched the carnage unfold in front of him and hoped that Timo would escape, Eron feared not only for Timo's life, but for his own. The realization that one day he'd face the same thing overwhelmed him, and when he heard the cries of his strong older brother, his spirit broke.

Eron threw his history book across the room. It slammed against the wall, knocking down a plaque he'd received for perfect attendance. Not like he had anything else to do with his time. The Selection loomed. He couldn't escape it. Much like Timo before him, he'd have to endure whatever happened. He only hoped the screams of his brother wouldn't continue to haunt him until then.

Three

About a week after the memories of Timo over-whelmed him, Eron found himself thinking again about his older brother. Eron couldn't shake the sound of those screams. He awoke one bright red morning to his brother's agonizing howls. Sweat ran down his forehead. His sheets were soaked. It took most of the school morning to finally push the haunting sounds out of his head. It wasn't until lunch that he could fo-cus on something else.

"Are you ready for the history test tomorrow?" Connor asked. He was a month younger than Eron, but slated for the same Selection. The Selection was held bi-annually and the boys had five months to prepare.

"Yeah, I guess so. I studied, but I'm still confused. I mean, it's not like it matters anyway. What do a bunch of old dead people have to do with me, especially if most of them were on Earth?" Eron said.

"Come on, Eron; it's more than that. We can't for-get our past. If we don't learn from past mistakes, we're more likely to make them again," Connor said.

"Whatever. That sounds like a line teachers cram down our throats! It's all worthless and you know it."

"Worthless? No way! It's serious stuff. Really. I mean it."

Eron rolled his eyes. Earth history didn't matter. Whatever happened years ago in some far-off world meant nothing to the Anastasians...to most, anyway. Eron couldn't think of a single good reason to study ancient Earth history. What had Earth done for them? Other than send the initial settlement and two follow-up missions, Earth had forgotten them. No messages, no resources, nothing. Anastasia was an afterthought. If that's how Earth thought of them, then why should Eron waste his time studying about Earth?

Anastasians stopped calling themselves Earthlings a century ago. The Earthlings obviously didn't care about them anymore, so why study their history?

"No matter what you think, you still need to be ready for the test," Connor said. He sliced a bright blue vegetable on his plate and popped a piece in his mouth. It was one of the few food staples native to Anastasia that wasn't poisonous to the humans and was packed with nutrients. They were cultivated in greenhouses on the far end of the colony.

"Hey look, it's Mina. Aren't you gonna say anything to her?" Connor asked. Eron ducked his head, pretending to give extra attention to his plate of food. "Eron, she's over there. Go talk to her!" Connor said, pointing with his fork and drawing the attention of the table next to them.

"Come on, Connor, stop," Eron said in a low voice. Not looking up from his plate, he waited for Mina to pass. "I don't feel like talking to her," he said. Connor shook his head and went back to his lunch.

Eron's heart raced. He'd wanted to talk to Mina for a long time, but just couldn't muster the courage. If Timo were here, he would have given Eron solid advice and encouragement.

Timo.

The screams.

He dropped his fork on his plate.

"I'm not hungry anymore. I'll see ya, Connor," Eron said. He picked up his plate and dumped the remainder of his food in the trash. If the lunch monitor caught him, he'd be in detention. Food was rationed and wasting it meant severe punishment, not that he cared at the moment. Let them take him to detention. It didn't matter. He missed his brother. Why did Timo have to go through the Selection? Why did Eron have to do the same? Why did any of them have to do it? And why not the girls?

His classes were a ten to one ratio of boys to girls. It had always been like that. No one offered an explanation of exactly what the Selection was or why only the boys had to participate. They spoke in generalities, saying things like, "It has to be done," and, "Every boy goes through it." They'd pat his head and smile as if it was the most natural thing ever. If it was, then why did Timo scream like he did? Why did Timo, his strong, energetic, unflappable brother, howl so fiercely?

Eron walked out of the lunch room and went outside. Shades of orange and yellow permeated the rich red landscape, the vegetation taking most of its color from the red sun that warmed the planet. A few laths flew above. Eron remembered learning about the creatures in history class. They were similar to birds and they could also swim for extended periods of time. The laths danced in the air, circling and darting around each other. Eron watched for a while, their sky theater a welcome distraction.

"You gonna stare at those things all day?"

Eron cringed. It was Bello. Bello was the same belligerent, loud-mouthed hulk of a boy he'd been in grade school that still got his kicks by picking on Eron. Bello was chosen for the second Selection as well. "Hi, Bello," Eron said. Timo had taught him to stand up for himself and treat Bello like everyone else.

Timo.

The screams.

Eron's mind drifted again.

"Why are you out here? Is it so I can kick your ass and no one will see it?" Bello said. Eron clenched his fists, ready for what came next.

"I'm out here because I want to, Bello. Shouldn't you be in class? You aren't smart enough to skip a lesson."

That set Bello off. He lunged at Eron, and Eron dodged his attack. Bello was huge, but Eron anticipated his moves. The two of them had tangled before. Bello fell to the ground. He leapt up, orange dirt covering his face and shirt.

"You'll pay for that, Eron!" Bello said. He feinted left and struck right, catching Eron square on the chin. A dull, heavy pain radiated across Eron's face. Bello didn't wait for Eron to strike back and punched him in the stomach. Eron tried to block the blows, and Bello punched him in the face again and again, staggering the boy, before Eron's fist could make contact. Bello held his hand to his face, checking for blood. Eron seized the moment and hit Bello several times in the stomach, though each shot was absorbed by the larger boy's girth. Bello smiled.

"That's all you got? I always knew you were a wuss.

Your brother had to fight your battles for you. Where's he now? I hear he got killed in the Selection. Serves him right. Your family has always been a bunch of cowards."

Eron's face flushed a shade of red deeper than the trees surrounding them. Spittle flew from his mouth. "Shut up, Bello! Timo was not a coward and he's not dead!"

Bello laughed. Eron lunged at the boy, slamming into him, but he didn't budge. Bello wrapped his huge arms around him and squeezed tight until Eron could barely breathe before he let go. When Eron bent over trying to catch his breath, Bello punched him in the face. "This," he said striking Eron, "is for being a coward and being the son of a coward and the brother of a coward." He struck Eron in the face over and over.

His will broken, Eron stopped fighting back. Tears streamed down his face, mixing with his blood.

"That's it! Cry, you little wuss. Cowards always cry," Bello said. He punched Eron one last time in the face and stopped. "I gotta stop wasting my time on cowards like you," he said and stomped away, leaving Eron hunched over, crying and bleeding.

When Connor noticed Eron wasn't in their next class, he said something to his teacher. A janitor found Eron outside, lying on the ground, curled in a ball. He was covered in sweat and orange dirt. Blood streaked down his grime-caked face like the red rivers that wound through Anastasia. After cleaning Eron up without getting out of him who'd beaten him so badly, the janitor walked him home. His mother opened the door, shock visible on her face. She left him alone that evening, sensing he needed space.

Four

Eron stayed home from school the rest of the week, building bridges and towers out of things in his room. He didn't feel like he'd miss much anyway. School days were only five Earth hours long, as dictated by the shorter daylight hours on Anastasia. Early settlers tried to mimic the twenty-four-hour, three-hundred and sixty-five day calendar of Earth, though they altered it soon after to accommodate Anastasia's faster rotation. February and September were the first months to be omitted; then eleven and twelve o'clock followed. Months were later renamed in defiance of the planet that neglected them.

A light knock on the door broke the silence of his room. "Son, don't you think you should get out of bed? Maybe go hiking or something? It's such a beautiful day out." Erin's mom waited for his answer. She held her hand to the door, hesitated, then left.

He ignored her and continued building a tower with his books, the largest ones on the bottom, tapering towards the top. One day he hoped to become an engineer and build marvels to rival those of Earth. If only he didn't have to take stupid classes like history, he'd have good enough grades to enter engineering school. If nothing changed, he was on track to join the agricultural branch of service, working in massive greenhouses growing food safe from the harsh Anastasian environment.

If he survived the Selection.

Eron spent the rest of the day in his room, day-dreaming of what might be. He imagined creating a communications system and using it to contact his dad. He tried desperately to remember his dad's face, but the image wouldn't crystalize.

Soon after, he fell asleep on his soft bed, hiding under a hortath hair blanket. He'd heard the older settlers say it was a material so fine it rivaled rabbit fur, whatever that was. The past expressions didn't mean much to Eron. They were holdovers from a time long gone.

When he woke, he rubbed crust from the corner of his eye. Anastasia's fine dirt permeated everything. Even with lush red forests and deep orange grasses holding tight to the soil, it was everywhere. Their in-home filter caught most of it, but now and then it got clogged and the dust infiltrated through every tiny crack.

Hunger forced him out of despair. Eron left his room in search of a snack. It was about five in the afternoon; the sun had already started dipping towards the surface and the house was strangely quiet. It was just him and his mom at home now. He was used to things being quieter than when his brother and sister lived there, but somehow it felt even more so now. The hum of the filtration system was the only sound and it seemed particularly loud.

"Mom?" he called out. She should've been home. "Mom?" he said again. He ran from the living room to her bedroom, then to his brother and sister's former bedrooms. The house was empty.

Rubbing his temple, Eron attempted to reorder his days. Was it Tuesday or Saturday? He couldn't tell. He'd been in his room so long, he'd lost track. Still, his mom should've been there.

The kitchen was clean; not a single dirty dish in the sink. No pots and pans on the stove. It was as though she'd never been there, and he knew that wasn't true. Maybe she went out. He hunted around for the note she surely would've left. After searching the whole house, he gave up. His stomach rumbled. He fixed a dish of fruit. The small, sweet red goibing berries were his favorite and the yellow farfell fruit's crunchy texture complimented them perfectly.

When he sat at the kitchen table, he spotted the note on the floor. How had he missed it? He picked it up and turned it over.

"Eron, I went out with Janyce. Be back soon."

Janyce was nice enough. Usually, his mom would go to her house to play cards or gossip about the latest happenings in the colony. Lately, they were stuck on a particularly spicy bit of news about Connor's mom. It was something Eron tried to ignore. Whatever it was, he didn't want to know.

With the mystery solved and his stomach full, Eron cleaned up the kitchen and went outside. The red sun had almost fallen out of view and only the last bright remnants illuminated the purplish sky. Eron hadn't planned to go far; just outside to enjoy fresh air.

He walked around his neighborhood of dome-shaped homes built out of native clay. They were all dark red, and each one of them looked the same as the one next door. The houses were laid out in a grid pattern with roads large enough to accommodate a military transport vehicle. Eron knew of cars from Earth's history, but other than military transports, he'd never seen one.

When Eron turned the corner, he almost collided with a pack of dire craates. They were one of the first creatures humans encountered when they landed on Anastasia. About one meter long and half that tall, their small bodies were covered in striped fur that varied drastically from a dull black and white to a bright blue and green. They were often easy to spot because they didn't blend in at all with the surrounding environment. No one understood why they had no natural camouflage, but fortunately they did. They were aggressive, especially in packs.

Eron stumbled and froze. The craates growled and hissed, baring their long yellow fangs. He took in the sharp talons they used to hold down live prey as they tore it to shreds while devouring it. Often, they left a trail of bloody carcasses behind. They preferred the wilderness and rarely entered the settlement. They were the dominant species on planet until humans appeared, and they did not get along well with their intruders.

Backing away slowly, Eron kept his eyes fixed on the craates. There were eight of them, enough to rip him to shreds and leave an unidentifiable pile of bloody bones. Each step he took backwards was deliberate. He raised and lowered each foot slowly so not to startle any of them. They growled, saliva dripping from their menacing fangs. He backed away about five meters when he turned and ran.

That was a mistake.

The pack of craates bolted after him; the howling, snarling beasts soon closing the gap. Running as fast as he could, Eron barely kept distance between himself and the lead craates. He could feel their hot, rancid breath on the back of his legs. They snapped at him, nearly ripping his flesh. Eron slowed. He'd never been physically active, and the long time spent sulking in his room didn't help. He had to find someplace to hide before they caught him.

Most houses were closed up for the night. He wasn't too far from home and decided to run for it. Hoping for the best, Eron broke into a sprint. The craates nipped at him. One tore his pants and almost brought him down. He tripped, but righted himself and ran faster. His small dome house was in sight. Bolstered by the thought of safety, he sprinted faster the last few blocks. His lungs burned. His legs tightened. Every muscle in his body threatened to turn on him, screaming in agony at their abuse.

Then he saw his mom. She was near the door, ready to open it.

"Mom!" Eron yelled. She turned toward him. The waning light made it hard to make out her features, but he thought she looked at him. "Mom, open the door! Now! Craates!" he yelled, exhausting his lungs.

He opened his mouth to say something else, but then stopped. It was either yell or run. He chose to keep running.

One of the craates broke from the pack, rocketing towards his mother. "Mom!" Eron's warning was too late. The craate was on her. Growing darkness made it hard to see, but he knew the craate was attacking. Eron

ran towards her, the rest of the pack chasing close behind.

As he neared her, Eron heard growling and snarling. The snap of jaws mauling his mother sickened
him. His mother sobbed and tried to beat the beast off
to no avail. It grabbed hold of her leg and twisted.
Eron lunged, knocking it off her. He sent it flying, but
it had ripped a chunk of her flesh in the process. It
landed on its side, yelping, then sprung at Eron. Steadying himself, Eron dodged its first attack before the
rest of the pack jumped on his back, knocking him
down.

Snapping jaws threatened his neck, hot saliva
splashing over him. He covered his head with his
arms, fangs tearing viciously into his flesh as they attacked him. His mother lurched toward them, her
arms swinging like pendulums. The beasts were unaf-
fected.

"Get off him!" a voice yelled. Howls and yelps
sounded in the dark. One by one, craates were ripped
off. Snarls turned to whimpers.

"Get out of here, you stupid animals!" the voice
said. The ravenous craates retreated.

"I told you your family was weak. I won't let anyone or anything else get you. That's for me to do," the
voice said. It was Bello. Eron's arms burned from the
attack. His back felt sticky.

"Thanks, Bello," he said in a shaky voice.

Craates.

And Bello.

It was too much to process.

"Where's my mom?" he asked. Bello pointed to a

dark figure on the ground. Eron dragged himself to her and was relieved to find she was still breathing.

"Next time, don't be so stupid. Or maybe learn to fight. You're gonna need to know how before the Selection, 'cause I'm coming for you as soon as it starts," Bello said. He stomped the ground, feinting an attack, then marched off. Eron watched Bello go, feeling an odd combination of relief and anger at him.

He tended to his mother lying on the ground. Her breathing was shallow. A nasty wound ran up her leg. Eron wrapped it in his shirt to stop the bleeding.

"Come on, mom, let's get inside." She didn't reply. Eron helped her stumble into the house.

All Eron could think of was Bello. And the Selection.

And Timo.

Brave Timo screaming at the Selection.

Could he handle it? All Eron knew was that he'd better be prepared, because there was no way out.

Five

After the attack, Eron spent several days in agony, burning pain emanating from the wound to the surrounding flesh. This was the major side effect of a craate bite, and humans had yet to create an antidote. The only thing they could do was to let it burn itself out. Everything they knew about pain suppression didn't help with a craate bite.

Eventually, the pain subsided and Eron could think straight. With his grades getting worse, he couldn't miss any more school. Bello left him alone, but being near him made Eron anxious. The coming Selection loomed like the tidally-locked moon. Every night, it reappeared, bright and pink in the black sky. Each day, the Selection felt the same way; always there and inescapable.

Eron's mom didn't complain about her craate bites. She limped but acted as though nothing was wrong. Eron didn't bring it up unless she did.

Considering Bello's words from that night, Eron worried even more about the Selection. He asked around, but no one would indulge him with information about what the Selection really was. The few remaining men in the colony were tightlipped when he approached them. None of the women had anything to say, other than, "that's just how it is."

At school, he approached one of his teachers, Mrs.

Stephenson, after class. He enjoyed her biology class, though his grade didn't reflect it.

"Mrs. Stephenson, can I ask you a question?" Eron said. The classroom was empty except for the two of them.

"Sure, Eron, what is it?"

"It's about...the Selection. I know I have to take part, but why? What is it? Why are only the boys part of it?"

Her eyes narrowed as he spouted his questions. She sat back in her chair with her arms folded.

"Eron, it's just something you have to do. It's always been that way."

"I know. Everyone tells me that. But there's got to be more to it. I don't even know what it is!" he said.

"How can you say that? You've been taught about it since you were young. I know you have. How old are you?"

"Seventeen Earth years."

"Seventeen? Then your time is approaching. Are you ready?"

"Ready? For what? What's gonna happen? No one says anything. I asked you because I thought you would tell me the truth. My mom won't tell me. My brother went through it already, but—" The screams were back in his head.

Timo, poor Timo.

"Timo, right?" she said. He nodded.

"He was a good student. Always at the top of the class. He studied a lot. You might want to do the same. It will certainly help you during the Selection."

"It didn't help Timo," he muttered. Mrs. Stephenson closed her eyes and bowed her head.

"I'm sorry, Eron. I didn't mean to hurt you." She looked at him and Eron thought he saw her eyes glisten. "Did I ever tell you about my son? His name was— I mean is—Nicholas. Nick was an average student. He loved to be outside. He was fascinated by plants and animals and learned everything he could about them. Actually, I'm pretty sure he knew more about nature than I do, and I'm a teacher! When he turned eighteen, he, too, had to go through the Selection."

Eron hung on every word.

"Nick went out with the rest of the boys at the Selection. It broke my heart to know I may never see my son again. Mothers are taught to expect it; taught that one day, it will happen. Watching him leave crushed me. My only consolation is the hope that his knowledge of nature served him well and he made it through."

This was more information than Eron had ever heard.

"You hope? You mean you don't know?"

Mrs. Stephenson shook her head. "No, I don't. That's another part of it. Your mother will also have to give you up. It's the most painful thing a mother must do, but it's how it is. It's an inevitable consequence of our being here. It's the price we must pay."

Eron's mouth hung open. Her words circled in his mind, drowning out everything else.

"Oh, I've said enough. You'll be fine. We all must face the Selection, though each of us in a different way. Remember that. You aren't alone. Now, if you'll excuse me, I have tests to grade." She waved him towards the door and he paused.

"Eron, you're not going through this by yourself. There are others. Look after each other."

Eron hesitated, wanting to know more, but Mrs. Stephenson had already turned to her papers.

No one had ever spoken so openly to him about the Selection; not that he remembered, at least. As a young boy, he was only told it was something he'd have to face later and nothing more. He figured the information was vague on purpose, but now he felt it was almost as if no one knew any details about it. Frustrated, he determined to find out on his own. Somehow.

Six

Eron spent his free time at school in the library, researching the Selection. Despite poor grades in history, he actually enjoyed the process of discovery. Connor came in to the library and sat down at Eron's table. Unable to find him at home after school, he figured Eron would be there.

Connor tried to persuade him to go outside and enjoy the warm breeze. Temperatures stayed mild year-round with a month or two of warmer weather in mid-summer. Lately, days were warmer than usual. Rumors spread it was a sign that Anastasia, the goddess for whom the planet was named, had declared it was time for the Selection. The Selection's timeframe was set in stone and not affected by changes in the weather or public opinion, yet people still whispered she was getting testy anyway.

"Come on, Eron, you spend all your time in here. How do you think you're gonna stand up to Bello if your nose is constantly in a book?" Connor said.

"Sorry, Connor, but I'm busy. I've got to know."

"Got to know? About what? The Selection? Didn't you pay attention in school? Eron, we both know it's necessary and inevitable. Why bother worrying over something that's gonna happen whether we fully understand it or not? You're wasting your time. Bello's gonna kill you out there if you aren't ready."

"Doesn't it bother you, Connor, knowing we might get killed? It's crazy! Nothing I've found tells me what happens during. Or after."

Connor shrugged. "I'm scared, too, but so what? People die all the time. At least this gives you a chance to get back at Bello."

"I can't believe you're ok with this. What if someone comes after you? Do you think you could kill another person? It's bizarre just saying it!"

Connor hesitated. "Yeah, I think I could. I'd have to. I want paradise. I want my choice of a beautiful bride. To live happily ever after in a land beyond. Just her and me, making sweet, sweet love all the time. Wouldn't that be great? Isn't that worth killing for?"

Eron thought about Timo. Someone just like Connor would've killed him and not thought twice about it. But what if Timo survived? What if he had to kill someone? Eron pushed his thoughts away. He couldn't break down now.

"I don't know if it's real, Connor. The paradise, I mean. How do we really know there are girls waiting for us on the other side? We don't know anyone who's been there. How do we know it's even true? For all we know, it could be a trap. I'm not willing to go blindly into something like that."

"Blindly?" Connor said. "We aren't going into it blind. We were taught survival. We have to be prepared for anything. Anything. No one told us it would be easy. We must be ready to kill or be killed. It's the law of the land. You know this. Don't you remember? What happened to you? I was in class with you when they taught us."

Eron shook his head. Why was this ok with everyone? Why was it only males that had to go through something so brutal? Well, at least he imagined it was brutal, but he had no proof, since no one ever really answered his questions.

"You think Mina will be waiting for you at the end?" Connor said, poking him in the ribs.

Eron smiled. "I hope so. I'd go through a lot to be with her."

"Then, you better start talking to her now! She hardly knows you exist anymore. Why are you so afraid to talk to her?"

"Whatever, Connor. Look, I'm gonna stay here and read for a while. If you want to stay, that's fine, but I'll be researching and keeping busy."

"I get the hint, Eron. I'll catch you later."

"Bye," Eron said. Connor left him in comfortable silence.

Eron dug through all the information he could get his hands on. The library's shelves held about five thousand actual tomes, and also had small electronic workstations called readers that were loaded with countless thousands more books and journals.

He spent almost three hours scanning articles about different topics, from growing crops and soil analysis to the occasional crime. The colony had an extremely low crime rate, which meant its police force wasn't large. There were ten officers to patrol a colony of about ten thousand. They often didn't have much to do. From what Eron read, Anastasia had always been this way.

"What about the Anastasian Defense Force?" he said out loud. His father was part of that, right? He thought so; it was what his mom had always said. He chased that thought, but after twenty minutes had passed and nothing came up, he returned to his search on the Selection.

As he was about to end his research for the night, he stumbled across a curious article.

An early scientist, Dr. Marsha Freulling, had discovered a virus not found on Earth and nothing like they'd experienced or uncovered previously on Anastasia. She described it as non-lethal but highly prevalent among female humans and almost non-existent in human males. According to the article, it was thought to be responsible for a list of ailments ranging from normal vomiting, dizziness, and fatigue, to more extreme cases involving death. Dr. Freulling implied that the female population was beginning to experience an adverse effect. She didn't expound on the idea, except to say that it was something to keep an eye on.

The article was short with very little detail, but something about it caught Eron's attention. His interest was piqued by the virus and that it only seemed to affect females. He'd never considered it, but for as long as he could remember, there had always been more males than females, and they were young males around his age or younger. Most all the adults were female. He found it strange almost all fathers were required to enlist in the Anastasian Defense Force. No one acted as if this was an anomaly and it never occurred to him to question it, but the article and the alarm Dr. Freulling had tried to convey spoke to him. Maybe there was a connection between the virus and the Selection somehow.

If there was, he couldn't process it. Reading all day had turned his brain to mush. He wrote down the important details in his notebook, intending to return to them when he had more mental energy. He was done for the day.

Seven

The next day, Eron decided to go outside. His room felt cramped and suffocating, and he needed to clear his head. He had a lot on his mind and the idea of getting away from everyone sounded perfect, even with the threat of craates. They weren't likely to be around. At least, he hoped not.

Packing a light snack of wheat and condria fruit bars, he set off. He could see the delight on his mother's face; she'd been trying to coax him out of his room for weeks.

Eron headed towards the Gorgia ravine, a lush valley east of the colony. Two rivers and several streams flowed from the mountains bordering the valley. He'd been there before with Connor and thought about stopping by to ask him along, but decided to go it alone. He'd rather argue with himself instead of listening to Connor's constant chatter.

At the edge of the valley, Eron paused, looking out over the vast expanse of wilderness. A few laths flew overhead. A large-billed hern streaked across the trees, darting after tiny insects. The sounds of the wild were intimidating but strangely comforting. It was as if the valley was a giant, living, breathing organism that welcomed him, yet held an undercurrent of malice. He'd always felt that way when he went outside, which was part of the reason he preferred to stay inside. That, and he hated the ever-present red dust.

The brilliant red and orange trees in front of him were interspersed with dull yellows and browns. Scrubby brush covered most of the ground with paths cut through it by earlier colonists. It was rumored there was a giant green redwood that grew in the valley. Apparently, it had been transplanted from Earth. He'd never seen it, though. Almost all Earth plants brought to Anastasia didn't survive. The nutrients in the soil were different, the native insects were destructive to most Earth vegetation, and the climate just wouldn't support the plants. Wheat was the only plant able to grow and thrive, which was a miracle for the colony and most likely had saved humans from extinction. Over time, they discovered several native plants humans could consume, though some early trials went horribly wrong.

Still, Eron doubted the giant green tree existed. It would've looked odd for sure. He couldn't imagine a tree or bush or any plant being bright green. It seemed weird to him. No plant should be that color.

He approached the nearest path and entered the valley's edge, kicking up dull red dust as he walked. It was midmorning and the red sun approached its zenith. In a few hours, it would be directly above him before beginning its long descent to the edge of the planet.

He followed the path up and down tree-covered hills and over one of the small streams that fed into the larger river deep in the valley. Red water swirled in pools and collected brightly-colored leaves as it flowed. He'd read that water on Earth was clear and oceans were a deep blue. They'd probably not know what to do if their waters were clear or blue. He couldn't imagine living in the strangeness of Earth. It didn't appeal to him. It was so different from Anastasia.

After crossing the stream, Eron came to a fork in the path. He walked left and soon heard the animal sounds cascading over him. It was the reason he came out here, to be surrounded by nature while trying to sort out his thoughts. He remained alert, listening for the sounds of packs of craates.

Eron's mind wandered. Timo's screams were the first thing to pop in his head. He closed his eyes and pinched the bridge of his nose. *Not now, Timo; not now.* Timo would have to wait. He couldn't spend his energy grieving again.

Thinking about Mrs. Stephenson and the articles he'd read, Eron tried to piece the puzzle together, the connections failing to materialize.

He sat down on a fallen tree to rest and eat his snack, when he heard a loud crash behind him. Jumping up and spinning around, he almost fell, but caught his balance. Tree branches were pushed aside as though something big was approaching. Crunching footsteps grew closer and closer. Laths scattered from the trees. The soothing sounds of the wilderness stopped, replaced instead with chittering and angry outbursts as the animals were disturbed. Eron didn't bring a knife or anything else that could be used as a weapon. Near his foot lay a thick, fairly straight branch that looked to be about his height. He grabbed it and held it in front of him.

Branches and smaller trees stopped moving. The

crunch of footsteps on the foliage fell silent. He heard a low, throaty growl. Eron couldn't see more than a dark silhouette through the thick brush. It looked to be about as tall as he, but broader. Eron's arms shook. The growl grew louder and more intense. His senses were on edge.

A twig snapped behind him.

Eron spun and swung the branch sword-like in the air. It smacked against a large tree, vibrating his arms as if thousands of bramble bugs were stinging him.

Nothing was there.

Behind him, he heard the crash of branches and the furious crunch of leaves as the creature emerged. Before Eron could turn, it slammed into his back, forcing him against a tree and knocking the air from his lungs. His nose went numb and a thin trickle of blood ran down his lips. He felt a heavy thump on his back, instantly sending a shock of pain across his shoulders.

"Get off me!" Eron yelled. He didn't have a clear view of what had attacked him. Out of the corner of his eye, he saw short, thick black hair on the creature's limbs. He turned to get a better look, but the creature grabbed his head with one hand and forced it away.

"No," the deep, almost human voice boomed. Eron's eyes went wide. His heart beat faster. There were certain animals that showed signs of intelligence, though nothing humanlike. This was something new. And frightening.

"I didn't do anything. Let me go!" Eron said. The beast held him against the tree.

"Don't turn around," it said, "or I will kill you." Eron nodded his understanding.

"Why are you out here?" the male voice said.

"I-I I came out here to think. That's all. I wasn't doing anything wrong," Eron said. Blood flowed faster from his nose and splattered on the tree as he talked.

"That's stupid. Do you expect me to believe you? I know you came out here to kill me."

"No! I didn't know you lived here. I don't even know who—what you are. Please, I'm not here to harm you."

The creature chuckled, dark and deep. "I'm certain you won't hurt me. You're pretty feeble for a human." It kept Eron's face pressed against the tree. Eron could feel the bark biting into his face. He didn't dare try to struggle against the creature's clutches.

"Who are you? What are you?" Eron asked. If he was going to die, he at least wanted to know what it was that would kill him. The creature pushed Eron's head harder into the tree.

"I am me. I am free. I am what you are, but better. That's all you need to know," it said. "I don't kill for sport. If I let you go, don't turn around. Don't try to get sneaky. Leave and don't come back. Am I clear?"

"Yes, yes you are. I won't turn around, promise," Eron said. His neck and back ached.

"And don't come back?" it said.

"And I won't come back, I swear. Please, let me go and I won't return."

The creature released Eron and it took a few steps back. "Go!" it said. Eron pulled away from the tree and ran, dropping the branch. He ran along the path toward the stream. Behind him, the growling grew louder and louder. Eron ran faster, wanting to put as much distance as he could between himself and the creature.

He ran, jumped the stream, and was several meters down the path before he couldn't hear the growling any longer. Feeling that he was far enough away to be safe, he stopped running. He bent over and heaved, spewing the contents of his stomach on the ground. When the convulsions stopped, he wiped his mouth and continued.

After what seemed to him to be an hour later when he was at the edge of the valley, he finally got the courage to look behind him. He spotted the large, dark, hulking creature in the brush about thirty meters back. Its features were obscured, but he knew it was staring at him. It had followed him all this way.

Eron ran home. As the sun set, he burst through the front door to a quiet, empty house.

Eight

Eron's mom was gone.

Again.

She'd go for a walk around the colony and leave him a note to let him know what she was doing, but this time was different. The back door of the house was broken and swinging open in the soft breeze. Overturned chairs and papers were scattered everywhere. Eron searched the house and found his room in shambles. His desk was a mess. It was as if someone tore through his research, looking for something in the notes and books and old maps. He noticed his notebook was missing.

Every room had been ransacked, his mom wasn't there. Something was wrong. He wondered if he'd stirred up trouble by researching the Selection and asking questions. Maybe the creature in the valley was a coincidence, but he wasn't sure. His immediate concern was to find his mother.

As he was about to search for her, the front door opened.

"Eron! What happened?" his mother said. She stood in the doorframe scanning the scene.

"Mom!"

Running to her, he could barely hide his relief. "I thought you were in trouble!"

"Trouble? I'm not, but you might be. What did you

do here?" She stood with her hands on her hips, scowling at him.

"Nothing, mom. It was like this when I got here." Clearing a place on the couch, he sat and crossed his arms. His shoulders ached.

"What's on your face? Is that blood?" she said. Eron touched the dried blood on his mouth.

"Yeah it's mine. I—"

"You what? Got in a fight with Bello again? Seriously Eron, when are you gonna learn?"

"It wasn't him! It was...something else. I'm not sure what. It attacked me in the valley. And spoke to me!"

"Son, don't be ridiculous! You have got to get your imagination under control. You know there is nothing out there but animals. And they don't talk." She furrowed her brow and shook her head. Then she spoke, her tone less angry.

"Eron, I know you're worried about the Selection. So am I. But it's something you have to do. Timo did it. You'll do it. If you have sons someday, they will also go through it. But worrying and making things up will not stop it from happening. You'll have to face it. There's no alternative."

Eron sat in silence, considering what to say.

His mom sat next to him and put her arm around him. Instead of pulling away, he accepted her embrace.

"I know it's tough, son. I promise you, if there was another way, I'd do all I could to get you out of it. But there isn't. You have to go."

"Mom, what is it? What exactly is the Selection? No one will tell me."

She sighed. "Son, I honestly don't know. I was on

the other side of it, where the boys go if they finish. We girls are chosen to be there according to compatibility. We don't always get paired and have to wait longer. I was waiting for your father there. He made it through the Selection. Not unscathed, but alive. I got to choose between two young men that came through the Selection; your father was one of them. When I saw him standing there with cuts on his face, he had a look of maturity and wisdom I'd never seen in him when I knew him before. It was at that moment I chose him. He graciously accepted my offer. I am forever grateful because out of our union, I had three wonderful children."

"He didn't tell you what happened?" Eron's mind sparked to life. He'd heard his mother talk before about choosing her mate; she'd just never told him these details.

"No, he didn't. I asked, though we were instructed not to. We were forbidden, actually. I couldn't help myself. I was curious. He never gave in, though. And after a while, I quit asking. It's just how things are, son. By the way, have you talked to Mina much lately? I know you've had your eye on her for some time. She's an excellent young woman, so smart and polite."

Eron looked down and didn't reply.

"Well, I suggest you do. When you make it through the Selection and she's standing there, you'd be lucky to have her choose you."

"But I don't understand—" His mom put her finger to his lips.

"It's ok, son, you don't have to understand. It is what it is."

She hugged him tight. It hurt his back and he

winced, but she didn't notice.

"Let's get this cleaned up. I might need to alert the police about what happened here. It's not normal to have a problem like this in the colony."

She cleaned the house as best she could. Eron moved slowly as he helped, more hindrance than assistance. When they got most of it picked up and back in place, he retired to his room.

CHAPTER

Nine

The next day, Eron couldn't wait to talk to Connor. When he finally caught up with him at school, he let loose with everything.

"Connor, a huge creature followed me out in the valley! It was covered in black hair and stronger than anything I've ever known. I've never seen anything so large in my life! It slammed me against a tree. See these cuts?" he said, pointing to his face. "It did this to me. Or he did. I'm not sure if it was an it or a he. But the strangest thing was that it spoke to me. Words!"

Connor's jaw dropped. They were sitting on a bench outside their school, waiting for the day to begin.

"No. Way," he said, then started laughing. "Eron, quit lying. I'm the one that makes jokes, not you. Don't let Mina hear you say stuff like that! She'll never choose you after the Selection!"

Connor laughed so hard that he doubled over, trying to catch his breath.

"Dang it, Connor, I'm serious! My mom wouldn't believe me, either. Forget it. Just shut up, ok?"

"No, I'm sorry. It sounds ridiculous. I'll stop. If you say it's true, then it is, I guess. Your mind hasn't been the same since..." he hesitated.

"Since what?" Eron said.

"Nothing. I'm sorry. I shouldn't have brought it up."

Timo. He means Timo. Eron balled his fists.

"Come on, Eron, I'm sorry. I didn't mean to upset you. I'm sorry."

"Somebody broke into our house. It was trashed."

Connor's face went white. "Crime? Here? That doesn't happen. We don't have those problems. Do you know who did it? Have you talked to the police?"

Eron nodded. "Yeah. My mom went to the station and they came out and looked around, but didn't find anything. They said we shouldn't have cleaned it up before telling them, but we didn't think about it. It's not like this kind of thing happens often."

Connor looked up and saw Mina walk by. He nudged Eron, pointing at her. Thinking about what his mother had said, Eron paused, then stood.

"Hey, Mina," he said. She stopped.

"Hi, Eron, how ya doing?" Her long reddish hair hung in curls around her face. The most beautiful golden eyes looked back at him and for a moment, he couldn't speak. Connor stood, bumped his arm, and walked away.

Eron snapped back to the present. "Um, oh. Hi, Mina. How-how are you?" he said. Sweat glistened on his forehead and his hands were clammy.

"I'm fine. Are you all right? Your face, I mean, how did you get those cuts?" she asked, pointing at his cheek. He ran a finger along the gash.

"This? Um, I...uh...I fell. I was hiking out in the valley and tripped over a log. This is a reminder to always pay attention to the details."

She nodded. "Seems like good advice to me. Maybe that'll help you in the Selection."

He opened his mouth to reply as sirens screamed to life. Students and teachers scrambled for the nearest storm shelter.

Their original settlement was about a hundred kilometers to the west, but was devastated by a sudden fierce storm and all but thirteen of the one hundred settlers were killed. They were caught off guard. Weather stations were built around the colony and manned by the Anastasian Defense Force to give advanced warning of impending storms by sounding the sirens. They had a short-wave radio network available to them, which was the only form of communication on the planet. It was strictly off limits for civilian use.

"Come on, let's get in the shelter," Eron said. He grabbed Mina's arm and led her towards a shelter near the school entrance where other students and instructors were gathering. The massive metal shelter doors were repurposed from the transport ships that brought humans to Anastasia. They were several hundred years old, but well-made and durable. Each one had a small window at eye level, perfect for watching the storm. A couple teachers closed and locked the doors with a heavy thunk just after Eron and Mina squeezed through. Outside, a massive storm cloud crept towards them. The menacing swirl of clouds and debris advanced, covering everything in its wake. When the storm was over, they'd be digging themselves out of red dirt for weeks. It was the reality of living on Anastasia.

Parts of buildings and trees and miscellaneous debris slammed against the doors. Eron cringed at the loud banging. He jumped back, bumping into Mina.

"Sorry," he said. She nodded. Holding tight to his

waist, Mina's touch made his heart beat faster. Eron peeked out the window at the storm. Through the howling wind and dust, he saw someone near the edge of the school grounds. He felt hot breath on his neck and turned to see Mina looking over his shoulder.

"Who's that?" she said, pointing.

"I don't know. But it's too late for them now," Eron said. A few other students crowded around the window, trying to see who they were talking about.

"Hey, that's Bello!" someone said. Eron cupped his hands around his eyes and pressed his face against the glass. It was Bello.

"Someone needs to help him!" Mina said.

"No way, we can't go out there," Eron said.

"He needs to find shelter fast, or the storm will overcome him," said a voice behind them. Eron turned. It was Mrs. Sharpe, one of the three science instructors.

A large tree slammed against the door, startling everyone inside. A girl in the back screamed. Eron looked out at Bello. The boy struggled to stay on his feet. Slowly he made his way toward the shelter, but the constant ravaging winds staggered him.

"He's not gonna make it," Mina said. "Someone should help him!" She nudged Eron. He froze. There was no way he was going out there, especially for Bello.

"Eron, do something!" she said.

"What do you want me to do? I can't go out. He'll need to take care of himself. If I go out there, then both of us will be in trouble. I can't risk it. I won't."

She stared at him, a look of disgust creeping over

her face. Eron had no desire to risk his life for Bello.

A click sounded and the door creaked open. One of the history teachers, Mrs. Brodey, dashed out in the storm, heading towards Bello. Debris flew around her. A large plank almost slammed into her head, but she saw it and ducked. However, she did not see the piece of the roof that had crashed down and smacked her in the back, knocking her sideways.

Eron was the closest to the door, and without thinking, opened it and ran towards her. Mina yelled. The fierce storm drowned her words. He looked back and saw her golden eyes staring at him through the window.

The wind lashed at him. Dust and dirt stung his face. He shielded his eyes with a hand and ran as best he could in the storm to help Mrs. Brodey. Large pieces of the building fell around him. Something struck his arm. He ignored the pain and went to where Mrs. Brodey was lying on the ground. When he got to her, her eyes were closed. He couldn't tell if she was alive or dead. He caught sight of Bello several meters away, swaying this way and that, turning around. To Eron, it looked like Bello was lost.

Bello wasn't that far away. If Eron ran forward, he'd get to him easy enough and could bring him back to help carry Mrs. Brodey to the shelter. Against his better judgment, he left his teacher and ran for Bello.

Not two meters from Mrs. Brodey, a piece of metal roofing slammed into Eron. It lifted him off the ground and carried him several meters east before dumping him to the ground. The impact resonated throughout his body. The wind shoved his face in the dirt. Sharp pain stabbed him in the ribs. Breathing grew difficult.

Choking on the mouthfuls of red dust, he rolled over and raised himself to his knees. Bello was ahead on the left, still fumbling in the storm.

Eron spat out the dirt. Steadying himself, he stood and carefully made his way towards Bello.

"Come on, this way!" he yelled. Reaching out to grab Bello's shoulder, he pulled the larger boy around.

Bello's eyes were covered in dust and dirt.

"What way?" he yelled back.

"Hold on to my belt! I'll lead the way," Eron said. With Bello holding tight to his belt, they made it back to Mrs. Brodey, avoiding larger chunks of flying debris.

When they reached her, she was covered in dust. A few more minutes, and she'd have been impossible to find.

"We need to get her!" Eron yelled.

"Get who? I can't see," said Bello. Eron bent down and scooped her up in his arms. She was too heavy for him and he struggled just to hold her.

"Bello, let go of my belt and help me carry her," Eron said. Bello let go and fumbled around until his hands found her. Eron guided him to a position that would help. With both boys holding on, Eron led them back to the shelter.

They reached the shelter and several students ran out to get Mrs. Brodey. Eron and Bello stumbled through the doors.

Ten

"Eron, I can't believe you went out there," Mina said. "Especially for Bello."

Eron sat in the infirmary, awaiting clearance from the med staff. The day after he brought Mrs. Brodey and Bello to the shelter, the storm finally let up. They had enough supplies to last a week, but they weren't needed. Mina and Connor took care of Eron's minor cuts, and though they did a great job of keeping his wounds clean, he still had to endure rigorous examinations from the med staff.

"Looks like you're all good, Eron," Dr. Kyle said. He was an older man, maybe sixty Earth years old.

"So, I can go now?" Eron asked. Mina sat in a chair next to the examination table, waiting.

"Yeah, you sure can. I understand your mother is on her way. Once she gets here, you can leave. Feel free to have a seat in the waiting room. She'll be here shortly."

Mina stood, thanked the doctor and left the room. Eron hesitated.

"Be right there, Mina," he said. She acknowledged him and took a seat in the waiting room. Eron closed the door.

"Soooo, Dr. Kyle, did you go through the Selection?" Eron asked.

Dr. Kyle stood against the door with his arms

crossed. "Is that what you want to talk about?"

Eron nodded.

"I see." Dr. Kyle looked down and closed his eyes. Rubbing his temples, he spoke. "I did go through the Selection. I had to," he paused, "do things. Not that I'm proud of it, but it had to be done. It's why I'm still here. You're almost of age, aren't you?"

"Yeah, in a couple months. Forty-three days to be exact."

"Are you ready? It's a challenging time for all young men."

"Dr. Kyle, what can you tell me about it? I don't have many people to talk to, and I'm worried." In his head, Timo's screams started quietly, as if from a distance, but threatened to burst forward.

"Other than to tell you that you must go through it, there's not much I can say. It will all be explained when you arrive at the station. Once there, you'll be given explicit instructions. I urge you to pay close attention. It could mean everything for you."

"But what does that mean? Why can't you tell me? Why is everyone so secretive about it?" Eron said. Tears formed in his eyes, but he was determined not to let the doctor have the satisfaction of seeing him break down.

"That girl," he said pointing at the door. "Do you like her?"

"Well, yeah...of course, I do. Why?"

"Stay close to her. It will help. Trust me. And just maybe she'll be waiting for you at Victory Point and she'll choose you." He winked.

Opening the door, he urged Eron out of the room.

"But you didn't answer my questions!"

"Oh, I didn't? Well, you'll find out soon enough. Be safe until then. You'll need your strength. And remember," he said in a quiet voice, "stay close to her. It's everything."

He ushered Eron out and closed the door behind him. By the time Eron made it to the waiting room, his mom had arrived and was talking with Mina. The two of them appeared to enjoy each other's company; a good omen, if Eron ever saw one.

The three of them walked home. Mina lived only a few streets away from Eron and his mother.

"I still can't believe you went out into that storm and saved Mrs. Brodey and Bello. I mean, you?" Mina said.

"Hey, give me some credit. I know I'm not always the first one lining up to face danger. I actually don't remember why I did it. I saw Mrs. Brodey, and something just...snapped. That's all I can say. I don't remember the rest. As far as Bello—-" he said.

"As far as Bello, what?" a deep voice said behind them.

Eron turned, Bello cracked his knuckles scowling.

"Go on, hero. Tell us. As far as Bello..." he said, holding out his hands as if expecting more.

"Bello, go on home, there's no need for this. Eron saved your life in the storm," Eron's mom said.

"Yeah, there is a need for this. I want to hear what this coward has to say."

"Coward? He saved your life!" Mina said. She took a few steps towards Bello, who backed up.

"Yeah. Coward. I want to hear his story."

"Look, Bello," Eron said, "I saw you needed help

and I helped you. Nothing more than that. You don't owe me anything, ok? We're fine. I'm glad to have helped."

"You're pathetic! You got lucky. I bet you were pissing your pants out there. I was fine. I didn't need your help. You only went out to make everyone think better about you. Watch your back. I will get you. If not now, I will in the Selection. I promise."

Bello looked at Mina and Eron's mom, shook his head, and stalked off. Before leaving he paused. "Oh, I heard about what happened at your house. Sucks for you. I wonder what they were after." He grinned and left.

Eron's mom watched him leave and turned to her son. "I'm so sorry, son. You did the right thing, even if it was for Bello. Keep that spirit alive in you, son; it'll help."

Mina hugged him. "You are the better man, Eron; I can see that in you. Your bravery is well noted."

Eron's face turned as red as the soil. "Thanks, Mina. And thanks for staying with me at the medic. It means a lot."

"Eron, why don't you take Mina home. I can make it from here. Are you well enough to keep walking?"

"Mom! Yeah, I'm fine. I'll see you later."

Eron and Mina continued towards her house.

"Eron, I do hope you make it through the Selection. I really do. I plan on being there, you know."

"You do?" Eron said. He stopped walking and looked at her, his head cocked to the side.

"Of course! My mom said it's the most important thing for you boys. I'll be there. I'll be waiting. Wanna know a secret?" A grin lit up her face. "I think I know who I'm picking," she whispered.

Eron's eyes bulged. "You do? Who?"

Mina giggled. "You'll figure it out. Hey, my house is here. Thanks for walking me home. Watch out for Bello." She turned, her long curls bouncing. Eron watched her go inside. It seemed like everyone knew something about the Selection except him. Even dull Bello knew more. How could he prepare if he had no idea what he was going to face? How could he not remember what he'd been taught?

Time was running out. If he didn't solve the puzzle soon, he might end up like...like...Timo. He couldn't let that happen. Timo was strong and smart, but something got the better of him. Eron was determined not to let that happen to himself.

Eleven

Eron spent the next several weeks researching as much as he could about the history of the colony. There wasn't much he didn't already know. Like how it once was called New Pasadena, but after the storm wiped out the first settlers, they moved to the new site and referred to it simply as "the colony." Or, how as far back as anyone could remember, male children far outnumbered the female children though once in adulthood, the number leveled off dramatically. He knew it was because of the Selection, but he didn't know what it was all about.

And he had two weeks until his turn.

Sleep eluded him as the fateful day approached.

"You look terrible," Mina said one day at school. The semester was nearly over, and though his mind was distracted, Eron still managed to pull his grades up and pass all his classes, to the delight of his mother.

"I know," he said. "I've not been sleeping well."

"The Selection?"

"Yeah. I keep thinking about it. I don't know what to expect. I have no idea what will happen. I do know that in a couple weeks, my entire life is gonna change."

Mina put her arm around him. "It will, but for the better. It has to be for the better, right? I mean, why else would they make you go through it? And when you get done, I'll be waiting for you. I promise." She kissed his cheek. He flushed.

They were growing closer by the day and it worried Eron. If something bad did happen, would he ever see her again? Thinking about that kept him awake at night almost as much as his worry about the Selection. As long as he could remember, he'd had a crush on her. Since the storm, they had become close friends and spent most of their free time together, when he wasn't doing his research.

"Thanks, Mina. I can't wait to see you there. But how will you know when I'm done? How will you know to be at Victory Point?"

She looked confused. "What do you mean? I guess someone will tell me. I can ask my mom. She'll know." Eron nodded. The bell rang and they went to class.

The next couple weeks continued pretty much in the same way. Preparations were underway throughout the colony. The houses were all decorated and special garlands of straw weed and granthium berries adorned those of the boys going off to the Selection. It seemed to Eron that every block had several boys participating. The day before the Selection started, Mina came over.

"Hey," she said when he opened the door. Her eyes were bloodshot, taking away from the gorgeous golden color Eron loved so much.

"Are you all right?" he asked after she sat down in the living room. "Can I get you something to drink?"

"No, I'm fine," she said. Her leg bounced gently and her gaze seemed distant.

"You don't look fine," he said. She fixed a serious gaze on him.

"Ok, I'm worried. I...I know now, Eron. And I'm

scared. Scared I'll never see you after tomorrow. Scared that maybe I won't be able to—" She placed her head in her hands and sobbed.

Eron sat beside her and comforted her. "It's ok. You'll see me again. I'll be fine. It's just some stupid ritual, right? I'll be all right." Her sobs grew louder.

"No, you won't. I know, Eron. I know!"

Eron's mom walked in the room. "Everything ok in here, kids? I thought I heard—" she said and stopped when she saw Mina sitting with her head in her hands. "Did she say she knew?"

"Yeah? So what?" he said.

"Out, now! Mina, I really like you and hope to one day be family, but right now, you have to go!" Eron's mom said.

"But mom, you can't do that! Can't you see she's upset?"

"I know, son, but she has to go before she says too much. Sorry, but Mina, you have to go. Eron, you'll see her tomorrow." Eron's mom held the door open, waiting for Mina to leave.

"Mom, this is crazy! You can't do this!"

"No, no, it's fine, Eron. She's right. I can't stay. I'm sorry. I'll see you tomorrow. Please, Eron," Mina said, touching his face, "be careful. For me." Her words hung in the air as she left.

Eron slammed his fists on his legs. "Mom! Why did you do that? You know how I feel about her!"

"Trust me, son. You'll thank me later. Soon, you'll have all the answers you wanted. And I'll be alone."

"I don't care about that! I care about Mina, and you ran her off! What will I do now?" He kicked a chair and yelled when it didn't budge. He'd feel that one for a while.

"She'll be there for you. I'll make sure of it, son. Trust me; you don't need to worry about her. Rest. You have a big day tomorrow. It's the last time you'll be my boy. After the Selection, you'll be a man. Then you'll be with Mina, or maybe someone else. Either way, things are about to change for you and me. We may or may not see each other again."

"Someone else? Not see each other? What the...you know what, mom? Forget it. I can't wait to get this over with." Eron stomped through the house to his room, slamming the door.

As he sat on the edge of his bed, contemplating the unknown, he heard the familiar sound of Timo's screaming from somewhere in the distance.

"Not now, Timo, I have my own problems." The screams silenced.

Twelve

The next morning, day broke like any other. The deep red sun rose in the west, its dark rouge rays brightening the dull red soil and vibrant fields of red and orange. Eron hardly slept at all. His mind was on high alert. The day had finally come.

Eron's mother awoke before he emerged from his bedroom and brewed a pot of cafke, and the sweet aroma permeated the house. Eron didn't care much for cafke, but this morning, he chose to partake.

"Here you go, son," his mom said. He sat at the kitchen table with the warm mug in his hands, staring at the steam.

"Listen, Eron, no matter what happens, you do what you must to get through the Selection. Do you hear me? Do anything you have to. Mina will be waiting for you. She's a great girl and you deserve someone like her. Make it through for her, if for nothing else."

Eron didn't move. He couldn't speak. His mind felt numb, as though covered in a heavy mist.

Eron's mom put her hand on his shoulder. "I know it's not easy, but I believe in you. I have to." She closed her eyes and squeezed his shoulder tight.

The unmistakable triple blast of the alarm reverberated throughout the colony. It paused, then blared the call again. It continued to sound for two minutes before falling silent.

It was time.

Eron's face turned white. A cold sensation started in his toes and rapidly worked its way up his legs and through his chest before intensifying in his head. The mug shook in his hands.

"Son, you have to go. The call has sounded." He pushed the cafke away and stood. In silence, he approached his mom and hugged her in a loving embrace. Comfort and warmth washed over him. There was nothing left to be said. It was his time. The Selection waited.

Eron left her and joined the line of boys headed to the far southern edge of the colony. Parents, neighbors, and relatives cheered them on. Some of the boys raised their fists like warriors and waved to the crowds. Others looked scared. Like Eron felt.

Mina stood at the corner of her street, her mom next to her. They cheered the boys on, and when they saw Eron, Mina yelled. "Eron, you can do this! I'll be waiting!" Eron raised a hand to acknowledge her words. She lowered her face and covered her eyes with her hands. Her mother wrapped an arm around her, drawing her close.

Nervous energy made the hairs on his arms stand on end. He didn't feel any calmer knowing all the boys were on the same journey.

Within minutes, he joined the group of boys surrounding a podium. He looked around and guessed there to be about fifty. In the center stood members of the Committee. As was the custom, there were three male and two female adults. Eron remembered this from Timo's turn at the Selection. As he stepped closer, he could hear their voices more clearly.

"This is your time, boys. When you are done, you will be men. But I caution you," said the man in the center of the Committee. The others deferred to him, and Eron assumed he was the chairman. "The Selection will whittle down your ranks. You must do whatever you can to survive. Survival at all costs, that's the key." In silence, he looked around.

"Guards, clear the area, please," one of the women of the Committee said. The crowd hushed. Armed men in dull grey uniforms ran behind the group of boys and forcibly pushed back everyone else. Mothers, girls, boys that were too young; all were moved back out of hearing range. Eron hadn't seen so many adult men in all his life. He wondered if his father was one of the guards. He hoped he wasn't.

When the area was clear, the chairman continued.

"The Selection was instituted to cure the problem of male overpopulation on our planet. In essence, it was created to drop your numbers. Look around you. Have you not noticed the large number of boys in your school? The Selection reduces the numbers. Many of you can expect to die. I hope you brought something to protect yourself. Many of you will never make it to the end."

There was an audible gasp. Eron's heart raced. So, this was it? This is what happened to my brother? He must've misheard the chairman.

"Some of you look at me like this is news to you. I hold your parents and teachers responsible for that, you should all be prepared. To those of you that make it through, Anastasian law forbids you to ever speak of what happened. You're all alive because your fathers survived the Selection and were paired with your mothers. This is not to be taken lightly. You are our future, however, there are too many of you. Our planet cannot sustain this."

The boys murmured to each other as an uneasiness crept through the crowd. Eron looked around, half expecting to see Bello grinning at him.

"Your job is to survive. The objective is Victory Point on Mount Jarrow," he said, pointing to the familiar mountain far to the south. It was forbidden territory, and now it was clear why.

"Once there, you'll be assisted in the pairing process. You have thirty days to make it. Show up a day late, and no one will be there. You will not be allowed to join the victors in the promised land. You will be forbidden to return here. You will be outcast as unfit. Forgotten. I urge you to proceed with haste."

Again, a low buzz grew among the boys as they processed what they heard.

"And finally, Selected, I caution you to be wary of beasts and animals and other hidden dangers on the grounds. You have plenty to concern yourself with in your fellow rivals, but dangers out there are real. Gentlemen," the chairman said to the armed guards, "please direct our Selected to the grounds."

The armed soldiers moved into action, herding them towards the edge of the forested grounds. They approached the edge of the rouge forest. Paths were trampled into the brush from years of use. The guards forced them to spread out, yet they were still close enough to hear each other breathing.

"From here, you will make your way to the other

side of the forest," the chairman said from behind them. "Let me reiterate. Your objective is to survive. At all costs. There is no other rule. You survive, and you get to live a long, natural life. Your fathers all made it through. Now, it's your time. Those who once were your friends should now be considered your competitors. This is real, boys. One mistake could mean your life."

The boys grumbled. Eron trembled. What exactly does he mean? Danger was in the air and Eron wanted out.

"And if you think you can run away and return home, you can forget it. Run, and the guards will shoot you immediately. They will shoot to kill. We've not had a defector in a while, and I don't anticipate one now. But just in case you've thought about it, I'd advise against it."

Eron looked to his left at a boy he recognized but barely knew. Ben? Kedron? Chas? He couldn't remember. The boy went to a different school and Eron had only seen him a few times. The boy's face was pale and his eyes were huge. He was shaking worse than Eron.

Eron considered saying something to calm him, but decided against it. The boy wasn't his concern. Surviving in the forest was.

"At the sound of the alarm, you begin your journey to manhood. There's no turning back. Your boyhood is over. When you emerge in the bright sunlight on the other side, you will be a man in more ways than you could've ever expected. Heed my warnings. May the great goddess Anastasia guide you and protect you."

There was a long stillness and even the forest seemed to listen to the chairman. The quiet stretched into a powerful silence. Perspiration ran down Eron's back. Every hair on his body felt electrified.

Then the alarm sounded and chaos ensued.

Thirteen

The frightened boy next to Eron stood motionless when the alarm sounded. He looked to either side and turned to run out of the forest. Gunshots filled the air. Bullets sliced through the foliage near Eron. The boy shrieked as they found their soft target. Blood splattered from the impact. His clothes were torn to shreds as the bullets ripped through him. He fell to the ground, lifeless, his blood pooling around him.

Eron paused, then ran into the forest as fast as he could. Tree branches pulled at him. Heavy, overgrown brush beside the well-worn dirt path reached for his feet. He heard screaming all around him. Timo. It all sounded like Timo. He pushed through the memories. There was no choice.

The forest grew darker as Eron ran deeper into it. Treetops blocked most of the sun's warm rays from penetrating, and the temperature cooled the farther in he ran. Still, he couldn't stop. There were screams all around and he didn't want to find out the cause. If he could make it out of the forest, he'd be done with this nightmare. He focused on Victory Point.

Eron ran on the path for quite some time. The screaming had let up and the feeling of impending doom had subsided. He stopped near a swiftly flowing stream and thought of being in the valley weeks before. He needed a weapon; something to protect himself with. A knife? The memory shook him. He forgot his knife. Frantically searching, he found a fallen tree branch that was large and straight enough to use for protection.

Howls and shrieks sounded again in the distance. Eron waited, listening.

"What's going on?" he said aloud. Watching the moving water, he tried to make sense of what he was seeing. The sun's rays poked intermittently through the orange and red leaves, creating beautiful streams of light. The beauty of the forest was quite a contrast from the uneasiness Eron felt. The sounds around him terrified him. After watching the guards shoot the boy, instinct was to run into the forest. Distant screams frightened him, though no gunshots sounded.

Eron waited, hoping to outlast the tortured screams. It didn't work. They echoed around him from every direction. He couldn't take the tension any longer. He grabbed his staff and followed the path before him, scanning the forest for other boys.

For the next couple hours as the sun rose higher overhead, Eron marched forward. A craate walking across the path in front of him startled him. Fortunately, it didn't turn to look or acknowledge he was there. Eron crouched with his staff pointed in its direction, ready to spring. He waited a long time before moving again. Seeing one craate was bad enough, but a whole pack was deadly. And they never travelled alone.

Hunger gnawed at Eron. His stomach rumbled. He realized they hadn't been given any rations. There were fruits and nuts in the forest he could eat. If he caught a squirm, he could roast it and eat it. "Fire," he said, realizing he didn't have anything to create a fire with him, either. Did he leave his fire starter with his knife? It was as though the boys were setup for failure from the start. How were they supposed to live thirty days in the wilderness without survival essentials? Death seemed inevitable.

Was that what the Committee wanted? Eron had a hard time accepting it. The colony needed as many able-bodied workers as possible to survive and thrive. Why would they intentionally kill off any of their members?

Hunger again called to him. Eron left the path in search of something to eat. There had to be a haynut tree somewhere nearby. He searched the ground for the thumb-sized nuts with elongated caps. They were easy enough to open and were edible, yet dull-tasting, but the tiny amount of protein would keep him going for now. He thought of how proud Mrs. Stephenson would be if she saw him using his lessons.

It didn't take long before Eron found enough haynuts to satiate the gnawing in his stomach. He filled his pockets with extras and turned back towards the path.

Except he couldn't find it. He was positive it was to the east of where he found the haynuts, but the trees and ground cover looked different to him than he remembered as he searched for the path. After walking for what seemed like too long, he went south, then north, but couldn't find his way back to the path. He was lost.

Eron's body shook when he realized his dilemma. Day one, and he'd already lost his way. No way to make a fire, no way to find the right course, no food easy to get. For a moment, curling up in a ball and waiting for the sweet sleep of death sounded appealing. "Get a hold of yourself," he said. "It's not even been a day! You can do this."

Night loomed. Getting a shelter set up or at least taking advantage of natural cover seemed like the logical next step. Eron scouted around and found a fallen tree that had landed across a log. It created a frame he could add a few larger branches and leaves to, and was the perfect place to rest for the night, hidden from the other boys.

Within half an hour, Eron had the shelter finished. High above him, the blazing red sun dipped towards the horizon, casting odd shadows in the forest. Eron hardly traveled into the valley at night. He'd heard too many scary stories of predators ready to attack. He'd have to be alert for anything wanting to harm him.

He settled under the shelter and covered himself as best he could. As twilight approached, the temperature dropped quickly. He shivered under the cover of sticks and leaves. He felt confined, yet exposed, as though any minute something would crash through and attack him.

Closing his eyes, the frightening sounds became louder. Sticks snapped. Leaves crunched. Something bounded across the forest floor. Laaths shrieking. Craates baying. His nerves were on edge. He tried to think of happier things, but his mind wouldn't allow it. Timo's screams echoed in his head. Then, the vision of the boy gunned down by the guards early in the day came to him. The rush of sound in the forest as the boys were let loose overpowered his thoughts. Where are the rest? Where are the other boys?

"Stop it! All of it!" he said, pounding his fists to the ground.

Behind him, a branch snapped. Footsteps drew near. His eyes grew large. Slowly, he reached for his staff and prepared for a fight.

Fourteen

"I thought I'd find you, coward."

Eron knew that voice. At once, he was both terrified and relieved.

Bello crashed through Eron's shelter, snapping sticks and scattering leaves everywhere. He tripped over a branch in the creeping darkness and fell on Eron, knocking the wind out of him.

"Stupid coward," Bello said. He pushed himself up and hovered over Eron, ready to exact his vengeance.

"Bello," Eron said in a low, wheezing voice, "please don't." He raised his arms in a weak attempt to thwart Bello's attack.

Outside the shelter, branches snapped and footsteps crunched around them. In the faint light, Eron could see the whites of Bello's eyes. The boy looked down at him. "You're on your own. I'd stick around to enjoy this, but I don't want any part of it. I don't feel like getting into it with those three. Not now. Good luck, coward!" Bello punched him in the stomach and raced out of the half-destroyed shelter.

"Hey, I'm over here!" Bello shouted. He glanced at Eron and grinned. "That's for you," he said and ran off. Eron could hear his clumsy feet smashing through leaves and brush, snapping branches as he went.

The other footsteps got louder as they headed towards him. If Bello was telling the truth, Eron was in trouble. He dug around in the remains of the shelter. In the back corner where Bello had crashed through, he thought he could hide under the sticks and leaves. It looked like only ground cover. In the darkness, he took the chance it would work.

Scrambling to get under the brush before the footsteps were on him, his heart raced wildly. Every sound in the forest was amplified in his ears. Faint in the distance, he heard Timo screaming. "No," he said softly and Timo stopped.

The sound of crunching leaves surrounded him.

"Where'd he go?" he heard a boy say.

"I thought the voice came from over here," another boy said.

They searched the area near Eron, poking the brush around him.

"I don't see anything," a third boy said. Eron didn't recognize the voices. Even if he did, he knew he wouldn't reveal himself.

"We better find him. If we let him go, he'll probably get one of us," the first boy said.

"Better to kill him first," the third one said. The shuffling around Eron stopped. They must've been listening for Bello's footsteps in the forest. Being so big and clumsy, he wouldn't be hard to track. Eron held his breath, hoping to conceal his location.

One of the boys stepped closer. Eron moved his arm slightly to avoid being stepped on and shifted leaves in the process.

"What's that?" the boy said.

"Shhh, we need to listen for him," one of them said. The boys stood motionless. Eron's blood rushed in his ears. Any movement now meant he would reveal himself.

"I lost him," the boy said. He walked away from Eron to regroup with the others. There was a loud thud and a louder yell as Bello fell over a log.

"Over there!" one of the boys shouted and the three ran after him.

Eron let out a deep breath. Sweat ran down his face despite the chilly evening air. Any movement earlier could've been his last.

They're gonna kill Bello? He'd imagined doing it many times back in the colony. As much satisfaction as he thought it would give him, he still couldn't bring himself to kill him.

Several minutes passed before Eron moved from his spot. Even though he could hear them running away and the sounds of their footsteps faded, he wasn't taking any chances. They said they were going to kill Bello. That meant they'd do the same to him. It was too great a risk.

The brush gave him a false sense of security, though if they'd heard him, he would have been caught. It was like getting out from under a blanket in the dark of his room. It didn't provide shelter or real protection, but once removed, he felt vulnerable.

Darkness had settled over the forest and the pinkish light of the moon shone. Eron listened for strange noises in the forest, preparing to hide under the brush again. Nothing sounded out of the ordinary. He looked in the direction where the boys were headed, but couldn't see a thing.

Not wanting to be discovered by another roving group, Eron gathered branches and large leaves to create a better hiding spot in the undergrowth.   Darkness would help, but the moonlight would give away anything not covered. After about an hour of preparation, he decided he'd done all he could do with what he had and crawled under his shelter, hoping it was enough to hide him from any predators.

Curled under the branches and leaves, Eron's mind drifted, hoping to comprehend what he was up against. If the goal was survival, it meant staying alert and ready at all times to do whatever was necessary to live. But that might mean hurting someone else, and he didn't think he could do that. Maybe if he was lucky, he wouldn't have to. He could try stealth and sneak around. It was better than confrontation. If Bello was running scared, how much more should he be worried?

Then his thoughts turned to Mina. Did she truly know what the Selection was about? Was she worried about him? Would he ever see her again? He hoped he would. Her beautiful gold eyes and long curly hair were burned in his memory. He admired her presence, so peaceful and confident. He had to endure to get back to her. What else did he have?

What about his mom? Why would she let them do that to her son...both of her sons? He punched the ground.

Timo.

She let them do this to Timo, and he was killed. Eron didn't see it happen, but the screaming began right after the alarm sounded. Like the boy next to Eron at the start, Timo must've turned to flee. Gunfire sounded and Timo's screams went silent. And their mom was all right with this?

Blood rushed to Eron's face, warming him.

Why? he thought over and over in his head. Why? He let the memories fade and the sounds of night took over. At some point, his eyes closed and he fell into a restless sleep.

Fifteen

The next morning dawned bright and noisy. Animals of all shapes and sizes scurried around along the forest floor, up in the trees, and in the air. The sounds were soothing and the warm red sun comforted Eron as it woke him from his sleep.

For a moment, he forgot where he was and marveled at his surroundings. Listening to the sounds calmed him.

Then he remembered why he was outside. And why he should be very, very afraid.

Peeking out from his hiding spot, Eron looked for signs of intruders. He couldn't hear anything over the din of the waking forest. Hoping he wasn't giving himself away, he shifted out of the shelter and stretched. Bones and muscles came alive.

He checked around, but nothing was amiss. He ate a few haynuts he'd kept from the day before and decided to go the same direction as Bello and the boys; if he was following them, at least he'd know if they were coming towards him. He'd also be headed in the general direction he'd need to go to get out of the forest and end his time in the Selection.

In the distance, he heard voices. He didn't know if it was the boys he followed or another group. He paused, listening. The voices faded and he continued.

Eron saw some trampled leaves directing him towards where the boys went. Following the path cut through the trees and small shrubs was easy, even for someone as untrained in tracking as Eron.

Small furry gracers played in the treetops above. They jumped from branch to branch, swinging by their tiny paws. Purple fur zoomed overhead as they leapt from one tree to another. They were easy to spot among the orange and red leaves, though they were quick. Eron watched the pack. All gracer packs were led by the largest female, who ruled without mercy. Weak gracers were left to die. Most males were ostracized and only the strongest of them were allowed to remain. The rest were chased off by the females.

Eron watched them and felt much like the male gracers. He wondered if there was a lead female directing the Selection.

He went back to tracking. Soon, he'd be close to the boys and would need to decide what action to take, if any.

The rest of the day, Eron followed what he thought was the path created by the boys going after Bello. By the time late afternoon set in, he still hadn't found them and grew concerned that maybe he'd gotten off track somewhere.

Haynut trees were abundant and Eron pocketed some of the tasteless nuts. The day faded to twilight. An overhanging branch off the path would serve as his shelter for the evening. With a few extra branches laid across the open area, there was enough shelter and protection. He settled in, and as darkness came over the forest, he drifted off to sleep.

Sometime in the middle of the night, he was awakened by laughter. Not two meters away from him were the three boys he'd been tracking.

"Ha, did you see his face when we ambushed him?" one of the boys said. He punched a tall blond-haired boy in the arm.

"Ouch. Dang it, Kumo, stop hitting me!" the blond boy said.

"Come on, Laird, it wasn't that hard," Kumo said. "Besides, you hit that kid a lot harder than that!"

All three boys laughed at Kumo's remark.

"Yeah, we got him good. His eyes were this big," the third boy said, making large circles with his hands.

"I know. It was awesome!" said Laird.

"Steen, did you see him wet himself?" Kumo said to the third boy, a shorter red-haired boy with a face full of freckles.

"Yeah. I almost had to stop, 'cause I was laughing so hard," Steen said. He made a motion towards the crotch of his pants. "It went everywhere!"

"Too bad for him, right?" Laird said. The boys nodded in agreement.

"It's better for us if we get rid of the rest. If we can make it to the end and eliminate our competition, we'll get the hottest girls and the best places to live. My dad told me that long ago," Kumo said. The boys quieted at the mention of Kumo's father. Many dads weren't around after their children were born. It was unusual to hear anything from them about the Selection.

"Your dad told you that?" Steen asked.

"Well, yeah, didn't yours?" Kumo said.

"No. My dad was long gone before I got to know him. He was called to the Anastasian Defense Force,

Cape Rouge Division," Steen said. Laird nodded.

"Mine, too," Laird said.

Eron listened intently to their conversation. They shared so many similar life stories, yet unlike them, he had no desire to kill. What made these three so cruel? As much as he hated Bello, Eron hoped he wasn't who they were talking about. It would be a shame if they got to him before Eron did. Not that he would kill Bello, but he planned on hurting him in some way if he could. Out here in the forest, there were no rules, no social conventions to stop violence. In fact, it was applauded and celebrated. The stronger you were out here, the greater chance of survival.

Eron moved his foot to scratch a sudden intense itch and shifted some leaves.

The boys shut up immediately.

"Hear that?" Laird said. "I told you someone was following us."

The boys remained silent. If they were any closer, Eron knew they'd hear his heart thumping in his chest. He tried holding his breath to keep quiet. When he exhaled, the still of the night betrayed him and one of the boys heard him.

"Over there! I heard someone breathing!" Kumo said. The boys walked straight towards Eron. He was about to reveal himself and beg for mercy, when a loud crash overhead stopped the boys in their tracks.

Streaks of green lightning raced across the black sky. Boom after boom reverberated throughout the forest.

"A storm," Steen said. "We need to get into the cave we found. Getting caught out here is suicide."

Kumo looked around once more. Eron thought for sure he'd been spotted when Kumo stared directly at his shelter. When the lightning flashed again, the boy's face was pure anger. His eyes seemed to glow as they peered right at him.

"Come on, Kumo, if that rain gets us, we're done for," Steen said. They ran off in the forest.

Steen was right. Eron knew the rain was dangerous, at least to human flesh. It was fine to drink after it pooled in ponds and lakes, but it was like acid as it rained down and landed on human skin. It burned and there was no way to remove it. The early colonists found out how dangerous it was after they landed here. It wasn't until the discovery of the planet's natural filtration system that the colony could thrive.

Eron knew if he didn't find shelter from the coming storm soon, he'd be as dead as the boy the others were talking about. Not caring if they caught him, he rushed from his hiding spot. He had no idea where to go. His only hope was to stumble onto a cave like the boys did.

Rushing through the dark forest, Eron pushed through thick shrubs and low-hanging branches. His face was hot as blood trickled along his chin where the tree branches scraped him.

Eron started to turn away from the approaching storm clouds and fell into a deep hole. He landed awkwardly, twisting his ankle.

"Oww!" he yelled, clutching his ankle. The sharp pain shot through his entire body. Writhing, he could hear the loud booms of thunder growing closer. Up above, streaks of green crossed the sky. He had to get moving again. When he tried to stand, the pain was too great. His ankle wouldn't support his body weight.

"No, no, no, no!" he said. He had to get out. He had to move. Sitting still would be his death. Crawling on his hands and knees, Eron scrambled out of the hole. There was nowhere to go. The thunder boomed again, startling him. It was much closer now.

He spotted a pithing tree nearby. The large leaves and thick branches created an opening large enough for him to be able to fit in. He crawled his way toward it. When he reached the low-hanging branches, the thunder grew in intensity. He dug into the ground. His hands ached and burned, but he couldn't stop. The storm was closer now. Lightning cut across the sky, and thunder boomed louder and louder.

Hoping to survive the storm, he crawled underneath the giant leaves just as the rain started pouring down.

Sixteen

The deadly rain continued for hours. Some of it dripped between the broad leaves overhead, but for the most part, Eron managed to stay clear. Small red pools gathered on the ground around him. Once the rain made contact with the surface of the planet, the toxicity evaporated and was no longer a danger to human flesh. Still, Eron took no chances. He was too far away from medical help to risk acidic burn.

When the sun finally rose, the rain stopped. The red dawn was bright and cheery in stark contrast to the dreary, deadly rain, and the life or death situation Eron found himself in.

South, Eron thought. *I have to go south.* That's where the promised land is. It seemed so far away. Here and now, deep in the forest with both humans and nature against him, the promised land seemed unreal. But it was his only hope. Going south was his chance to live...assuming he survived the forest.

Eron rested under the tree until midday when the red sun had burned most of the rain away, leaving the air thick and heavy. He needed to get moving if he wanted to make it to Victory Point.

When he stood, Eron found walking difficult because of the tumble he'd taken the night before. He leaned on his stick for support and limped on, hoping not to cross paths with the boys or Bello.

Eron found a fast-moving stream and drank of the cool red water. With his eyes closed, he savored the liquid, letting the refreshing chill invigorate him. He opened his eyes as some shrimp swam by. Other than their size, they were nothing like the shrimp on Earth. The early colonists couldn't think of another name to call the small creatures with two large tails and ten legs. The tiny creatures darted around the bed of the stream, rolling pebbles and sticks toward the banks. They climbed out of the water, pushing the pebbles and sticks against mud structures that were formed along the far side of the stream. There were four of them in a row standing about ten centimeters tall. Eron wondered what they were.

He watched them as he sipped the cool water, wondering how easily he'd be able to catch one to eat. When he dipped his hand in the water, they scattered and he realized they were probably too quick.

He heard shouting in the distance. Jumping up and ignoring the pain in his ankle, Eron strained to hear the voice.

"Help!" someone yelled. "Help me! They're trying to kill me!"

Eron hesitated. He was in no shape to help anyone, but he thought of Timo. What if Timo had called for help and no one came? His brother screamed softly inside his head.

Using his stick to stay upright, Eron wobbled towards the commotion, trying to stay hidden and as quiet as possible.

"Help!" he heard again and again. When he was close enough to take a peek without being observed, he gaped at what he saw.

There was a boy clinging to the branches of a tree. Craates circled below, snarling and snapping their jaws. But the craates weren't what caught Eron's attention. It was the boy.

He was blue. With dark green hair.

Everyone in the colony had fair skin. Hair colors ranged from red to yellow to orange, and even brown, but never green.

And never blue skin.

The boy clung to a branch that sagged under his weight. To Eron, it looked like a matter of time before the craates would have their prey. Desperation in the boy's cries for help forced Eron into action.

Three craates waited at the bottom of the tree. Eron used his stick to rustle the bushes around him. The craates stopped and turned his way. He made another noise with his stick and one of the craates approached with fangs bared, staying low to the ground. Saliva dripped from its mouth with each step.

As the craate poked its head in the bush, Eron brought his stick down hard. A sickening crunch sounded as the stick collapsed its skull. It was dead in an instant.

One of the other craates whined, then ran snarling toward Eron. It leapt over the bush, surprising him, and crashed into his shoulders, knocking him to the ground. It snapped at him with large yellow fangs. Eron held it by the neck and squeezed. It thrashed back and forth, trying to bite his hands. Eron's knuckles turned white as his grip around its neck held. The eyes of the beast narrowed while Eron's hands closed tighter and tighter around its neck.

It snapped at Eron's hands, but they were out of reach. Just as Eron thought he'd killed it, the third craate bit his leg and he let go. It fell to the ground next to him, gasping and pawing wildly.

A sharp pain radiated from the bite and Eron screamed, holding his leg. Another sudden bite sent more sharp streaks of pain through his leg. Eron kicked, trying desperately to get the thing away from him.

The craate next to him regained its strength and leapt on him, pinning Eron to the ground. It growled as it stood over him and snapped at his face. Eron pushed against its chest, holding it back, but his grip weakened as it strained to bite him.

He heard a yelp near his legs, and out of the corner of his eye, Eron saw the craate that had been beside him go flying. The one above him snapped at his nose, missing by a centimeter or two. Then its eyes rolled back and the body went limp in his hands. He tossed it aside and saw the blue boy with a bloody knife in his hands.

"You all right?" he asked Eron.

Hot, searing pain shot through Eron's leg.

"Yeah, just got bit; that's all. Hurts, but, you know. It goes away."

"Thanks for the help. They surrounded me and I dropped my knife so I climbed up the tree. I had no idea how to get away. Thanks so much!"

The boy paused and pointed his knife at Eron. "Hey, wait. You're not one of them, are you? Those boys trying to kill me? I'll gut you right now if you are!"

"I heard you calling for help and came to see what I could do. I'm not gonna hurt you, I swear!" Eron said. He held up his hands to show he meant no harm.

The boy scowled, then sheathed his knife and extended his hand to help Eron up.

"You try anything, and this knife will go in your belly," he said patting the sheath. Eron nodded.

"My name's Phelan. What's yours?" he said.

"Eron. My name is Eron. I'm here for the Selection. Why are you here?"

Phelan smiled. "The same thing. What are you, dense?"

"No. It's just...I've never seen anyone like you before."

Phelan lowered his head. "Yeah, well I'm as real as you are."

Seventeen

"Our colony has been around since humans first stepped foot on this planet," Phelan said. "It was cut off from the rest of them. It seems the founding settlers wanted it that way."

Eron limped along the path as they headed south. He kept some distance between the two of them in case Phelan tried to attack.

"Wait," Eron said. "You said the rest of them? As in, there are other colonies besides mine and yours?"

Since he was a boy, he'd been taught his colony was the only one on Anastasia. But colonies other than his own? And other races? He was taught about the far side of the colony and nothing more.

"Well, yeah. There are five different colonies. Mine is Greater Manthus, yours is Rippon, and then the other three are Banthium, New Anaheim, and Cape Rouge. They surround this forest."

Eron was confused. He had grown up in the colony—Rippon, as Phelan named it, and no one had ever called it anything other than "the colony." No name was given to it. No sense of identity.

"How do you know all this?" Eron asked. Phelan giggled.

"From school! How else would I know? Aren't you taught the same things?"

Eron looked toward the sky, his eyebrow arched. "I

guess not. We're told our colony is the only one. There was never a question of whether there were others or not. Humans came to this planet and settled our colony, end of story. At least that's what I remember."

"Obviously, it's not the end of the story, is it? I mean, I'm here. Greater Manthus is here. All the other colonies are here. I don't know what they actually teach you in Rippon, but it's not the truth. I wonder what kind of place Rippon really is. We were all strangers on this planet, trying to create a new way of life, not carry on the legacies that forced us off Earth to begin with."

"Where was your starting point for The Selection? I thought I was where it began."

Phelan smiled. "Our starting point is on the far east side of the forest. All the colonies border the forest and have the same distance to travel to Victory Point."

Eron closed his eyes and leaned on his stick. His ankle hurt and now his head hurt, too. Was Phelan right? Were they lying to them in Rippon? Why? Maybe this new boy was the one lying, trying to confuse him.

When Eron opened his eyes, he stared at the back of Phelan, who'd kept walking. The blue skin and green hair mesmerized him. Phelan took a few more steps before turning around and catching Eron looking at him.

"What? Haven't you ever seen a blue human before?"

"Umm, well..." Eron said.

"Really? You've never seen anyone look different

than you? There are all kinds of us out here. Not just pale and blue." Phelan shook his head.

"Phelan, I don't know what to say. I only remember being taught certain things. We left Earth so long ago, and we don't call it home anymore. We're Anastasians now. I assume you are, too, but I'm not too sure right now."

"You're gonna question my heritage? Why? Because my skin is blue?"

"Come on, Phelan, don't get so upset," Eron said.

Phelan took a few steps and turned.

"It's people like you that forced us into our own colony to begin with," Phelan said. His voice was barely above a whisper. "I know you saved me, and I appreciate it. Honestly, I ought to kill you before you do the same to me. But somehow, I get the feeling you won't, so, I'll be nice. For now. If you plan on sticking with me, you better watch yourself. I won't tolerate ignorance. And if you don't carry your weight, I just might kill you."

Eron considered his words. "Yeah, I got ya. You don't seem like the type to do something bad to me, either. Keep your distance, though; I can't be too sure."

Phelan laughed. "Yeah, whatever you say. We need to find shelter before nightfall. Maybe you can tell me a bit about yourself on the way. I've not been around too many people from Rippon."

The two boys continued through the forest and talked about friends, the colony, and their families. Phelan was an only child. Eron choked up when he talked about Timo departing for the Selection.

"So, is he dead?" Phelan asked.

"I think so, but I don't know for sure. I mean, yeah,

I guess he is. How could he not be?" Phelan stopped for a moment and gave Eron a serious look.

"What?" Eron asked.

"Maybe he's still alive. He could be. Unless you see a body, always assume he's alive. At least, that's what I say."

"What goes on in Greater Manthus? Why would you have a saying like that?"

"Never mind. I just think maybe you shouldn't forget about him yet."

"Like that's gonna happen. I hear his screams all the time. They haunt me," Eron said.

Phelan let the subject drop, much to Eron's delight. The boys built a shelter near a large tree and settled in for the evening, snacking on Eron's haynuts and griffle berries Phelan found earlier.

"How about we take turns keeping watch?" Phelan said. Eron was exhausted and welcomed the rest.

"How do I know you won't kill me in my sleep?" Eron asked.

"You don't," Phelan said grinning. "You'll just have to trust me."

Eron didn't reply. Phelan didn't appear too threatening, yet all it would take was one mistake, and his life was over. Eron didn't like those chances. He sat against a tree facing Phelan, intending on staying awake to keep an eye on him. With his eyes partially closed, Eron pretended to sleep while watching Phelan. Much to Phelan's credit, he didn't try anything, and it didn't take long for Eron to pass out.

———

"Hey, wake up. It's your turn," Phelan said, shaking Eron by the shoulder. The blue face looking at him in the moonlight startled him and wakefulness slammed into him.

"What! Who?" and before he could grab his stick, he realized who it was and calmed down.

"You've been sleeping for a few hours. I'd like to get some rest before tomorrow, too," Phelan said. Eron nodded and the boys switched places.

"How do I know you won't kill me?" Phelan asked with a smile.

Eron replied, "You don't. You'll just have to trust me." Phelan leaned against the tree, and in minutes was snoring lightly.

By the time the sun rose, both boys were awake and again on their way south, seeking the promise of a better life.

Eighteen

Not long after starting their day, the boys discovered a mutilated corpse near a large tree. The skin was dark brown and the face was unrecognizable. Blood had dried on the ground around it. The torso had been ripped open, and entrails and organs were strewn over it.

Eron immediately emptied the meager contents of his stomach. Phelan paled, but controlled the urge.

"What did this?" Eron asked after he recovered.

"I'm not sure. Think it was other boys? He looks terrible."

"The way the insides are torn out makes me think it was something else," Eron said. "If it was other boys, I don't want to get near them."

Phelan looked at Eron, then stooped to check the body for anything useful. "Hey look," he said pulling out a large knife from the belt of the bloodied and desecrated body.

"Lot of good it did him," Phelan said. "Maybe we'll do better. Here, you take it. I have one already."

Eron hesitated, then tucked the knife in his waistband. It felt vile, but it was a weapon. If he had learned anything so far, it was that he couldn't turn down something as valuable as that.

To their left, a deep growl startled the boys.

"What was that?" Eron said. He grabbed the knife

and steadied himself with his stick.

Phelan spun toward the sound. "I'm not sure."

The growls grew more menacing. Leaves crunched as something shuffled towards them.

"You're in my home now. Soon, you'll die," a deep human voice said. A large humanoid emerged from behind a tree. It was covered in short, thick black hair.

"Hey! I've seen one of these before," Eron said. "I stumbled across it in the valley near my colony. It was strong. It almost killed me."

"One of the Forgotten was that close to you? They stay here in the forest. If any of them try to escape, they're shot!" Phelan replied.

"The Forgotten?" Eron asked. Phelan didn't have time to reply. The creature approached them with arms raised, growling.

"Get out of my home!" it said. It swung its huge arms from side to side, clearing a path for itself. Small branches and bushes snapped in its wake. Eron held the knife toward it with a shaking hand. Phelan un-sheathed his knife and took a few steps to the side.

"I've warned you boys many times never to come in here. Never! And you don't listen," it said. It was only a few meters away.

With a quickness neither boy anticipated, the crea-ture rushed at Eron. It slammed into him, lifting him off the ground and knocking him back a meter or two before he crashed into a tree. The knife flew from his hands and his stick snapped as the creature stepped on it. He struggled for air, gasping and wheezing.

Phelan lunged at it, only to be brushed aside as though he were a pesky insect. The boy jumped up and struck again. The creature roared and swung each fist at Phelan, catching him first with its right and then its left in the stomach. Phelan bent over, clutching his abdomen.

Eron struggled but finally caught his breath.

"Please, we don't mean any harm. We're forced to be here. We had no choice," he pleaded with the beast.

"Shut up! I've warned all of you to never come back again!" It lunged at Eron, knocking him down. It punched him in the stomach and face. Blood trickled out of Eron's nose and his upper lip swelled and burst open, blood filling his mouth.

"Never come here! Never come here!" it screamed at Eron. Phelan lunged with his knife. The beast raised one large paw and swatted the attack away.

"Get off him!" Phelan yelled. "We have to be here. Just like you did once! Let him go!"

Phelan lunged again, aiming lower this time, stabbing the creature in the back of its leg. The blood-curdling howl filled the forest.

It let go of Eron and swung, striking Phelan across the face. His head whipped back and blood spilled from his mouth. Eron saw a chance and kicked the creature, hoping to catch it where Phelan's knife was lodged in its leg. He was close enough and the thing roared. Both boys covered their ears against the thundering bellow.

The beast leapt on Eron, pounding him with its heavy paws. It growled and spat on him. Eron tried the best he could to block the blows, but the beast was unrelenting. Eron saw its eyes glaze over, as though in a trance. Blow after blow landed on him, bursts of pain exploding through his body.

Phelan swayed from side to side. He fell to the ground and forced himself up. Between punches, Eron saw his new friend stumble toward the creature. A paw raised and Eron saw Phelan move closer. A paw slammed down and Eron closed his eyes with the punch. He opened his eyes. With its paws poised to strike, he saw Phelan plunge his knife into the creature's back.

Its eyes regained life and it roared in pain. It flailed, trying to remove the knife stuck in its back. Phelan shoved it in further and twisted before being knocked backwards. With much effort, Eron kicked up and pushed the creature off him. It fell, still struggling. Both boys moved away as it tried in vain to remove the knife. Jumping up, it stumbled around wildly, flailing as if still trying to attack them, but they moved farther and farther away.

With a deafening scream, it ran into the forest, crashing through bushes and low-hanging branches.

Phelan dropped to the ground. Eron leaned against a tree. Exhaustion overwhelmed them.

"What was that? Eron asked.

Phelan looked at him, his face haggard. "Come on, we need to go before it returns."

Nineteen

Eron and Phelan left the corpse. Insects had infested it. Eron wanted to bury it, but after their fight with the creature, Phelan decided it was best they move on.

Both boys were hurt. Phelan had a gash on his lip as did Eron, and Eron's bruises were coloring. Their bodies ached.

"My knife!" Phelan said.

"What about it?"

"It was still stuck in that beast's back!"

Eron fumbled for his knife and handed it to him. "Here, take mine. I didn't do so good with it. Maybe you'll have better luck."

Phelan took it and tucked it in the waistline of his pants.

"What was that thing?" Eron asked. It was his second encounter with the mysterious creatures, and still he had no idea what they were.

"The Forgotten? The lost ones? Didn't you learn about them? Probably not."

Eron shook his head.

"They're us. Or they used to be someone like us. They are boys who never made it out of here and weren't killed in the Selection. They get stuck here. Over time, they turn into those creatures. I think the planet itself reclaims them into a primitive state of some kind, or something like that. It's like reverse engineering or reverse evolution. I don't know how to describe it. But you get what I mean," Phelan said.

Eron leaned on the new staff he'd picked up after the creature crushed his other one. He stared at Phelan. "Do you think my brother is one of those things? One of the Forgotten?"

"Well, if he never made it out and is still alive, then I guess it's possible. I wouldn't get too excited about it, though. Once they're Forgotten, they never come back. They're more deadly than a pack of craates. Come on; we need to keep moving." Phelan wiped at his mouth with his hand. The red blood left a purple smear on his blue skin.

After walking a bit, Eron slowed and collapsed on the ground.

"Are you all right?" Phelan said.

"Yeah, I'm fine. I'm tired. I feel weak."

"We need some food. I'm getting tired, too. Maybe we should stay here and rest. We still have twenty days left to find Victory Point or become one of the Forgotten," Phelan said.

"Twenty? How do you know? I can't remember how long I've been out here."

Phelan tapped a long blue finger against his temple. "I remember. I count the days, like you should've been doing! Don't they prepare you at all in Rippon?"

Eron hung his head. "No, no, they don't. Well, maybe they do, but I wasn't prepared. It doesn't make sense. I mean, all of this. The Selection is pointless. Why send us out here to die? Why the big ordeal?"

"The Selection is a solution to a problem. We have too many males on Anastasia. Always have had since the first colonists arrived. Some believe it was a plot by the original governments of Earth; a cruel lesson to the colonists for leaving. Others say the planet affected human genes, altering them to create more males than females. I don't know which story is true. Whatever the reason, the population is out of balance, and it has to be restored."

"What the...that sounds crazy!" Eron said. He crawled to a nearby tree and rested against it, regarding Phelan with his brows furrowed.

"Call it what you want, but that's the case. In every colony, young males outnumber the females at least ten to one."

Eron shook his head. "It doesn't make sense. Wouldn't it be easier if they just killed the boys early on? Why raise us only to send us off to die. Seems like a waste."

"You make sense but I don't have an answer. You can whine about it if you like. Sulk, too, but it won't change anything. It is what it is, and we have to deal with it. I'm not thrilled, either, but it's our fate."

"Fate," Eron repeated, his gaze distant.

"Let's get some rest. I'll take the first watch," Phelan said. Soon, Eron drifted off to a deep sleep.

Twenty

*"Eron, I miss you. You look so tired. Are you all right?"
Mina said. Eron stared into her golden eyes, marveling at
her beauty. She was more stunning than he remembered.
Her hair bounced as she talked and her smile melted
away all his frustration.*

"Yeah, Mina, I'm ok. Sort of. I'm a little hurt, but it's
nothing serious. I'll be fine soon. I met someone."

"Someone? A girl?"

"No, not like that. I met another guy. Except he's blue.
Have you ever seen a blue person before?"

Mina smiled. "Well, of course I have! Everyone knows
they live in Greater Manthus. They've been there since
humans landed on Anastasia. They're different, that's
why they were sent there. Didn't you pay attention in
school?"

"I guess not. But I found him in a tree. I helped him to
avoid a craate attack. I helped him. You should've seen
me."

"I bet you were the great hero I know you can be,
Eron. I'm waiting for you. I'll be there at the end when
you wake up. When you get up, I'll be there. I promise. All
you have to do is wake up..."

"Wake up, Eron! Get up!" Phelan shook Eron. "Get
up, we've got company," Phelan said in a low voice.
Eron scrunched his face and was about to speak when
Phelan held his finger to his lips and shook his head.

Eron nodded and sat up as quietly as he could.

Phelan pointed east. The first rays of the morning sun were peeking over the horizon. Bright red streaks swept across the sky. Eron squinted and held his hand over his eyes. Twenty meters away, he saw a person. Two others followed slowly behind.

"Stay quiet. Maybe they won't notice us," Phelan said.

Eron couldn't turn his gaze from them. The hairs on the back of his neck stood straight out. A chill ran through his body.

"I say we follow them. Best to know where an attack is coming from. If we can keep our distance but keep them in sight, we'll stand a greater chance of not getting caught," Phelan said.

"I'm not so sure about this, Phelan. I mean, that's kind of dangerous, don't you think? Why don't we just let them go and wait a while before moving?"

"Eron, this is a perfect opportunity to get rid of our competition. Well, some of them, anyway. If we don't do this, they're more likely to get us. And they have the advantage with numbers. If we can catch them off guard and strike when they least expect it, maybe we can even out the odds or turn them in our favor."

Phelan bounced as he sat back on his feet. He fidgeted with a small stick, stabbing at an invisible foe.

"I don't know, Phelan. We're not in any shape to attack anyone. It's not like we need to. If we let them go, maybe they'll leave us alone, too."

Phelan turned to Eron. The red sun's rays brightened his blue face, making him appear angry.

"You do know they can and probably will kill you if

they catch you, right? There are no rules out here. The Selection is every man for himself. If you survive, you're rewarded. If you don't, then it's because you weren't strong enough or smart enough to figure out what needed to be done."

Eron closed his eyes and thought of Mina. Her voice sang in his ears. The way her eyes lit up when she talked to him, the way her hair curled. He imagined her reaction at the end of the Selection if he wasn't there. The disappointment on her face. Anger and disgust at the lack of the man Eron turned out to be. His mom standing next to her, apologizing for him.

"Ok," Eron said. His teeth were clenched and his voice was quiet. "We can do this. I don't feel right about it, but you're the one who knows more about what's going on. I'll do anything to get back to Mina."

"That's it, Eron! Come on, let's get going before they get too far ahead."

The boys watched as the figures moved slowly across the forest. They crouched low and went from bush to tree, hiding as best they could. Phelan took the lead and motioned to Eron when to move and when to remain still. He waved his hand and pointed to a large tree. Eron lurched his way forward, hoping his awkward gait didn't give them away.

They stalked them for close to an hour. The lead boy was taller than the other two, and one of the boys lagging behind was limping as the other tried to help him along.

Phelan motioned for Eron to stay put as he crawled on the forest floor, going from cover to cover until positioned dangerously close to the boys. For a moment, Eron thought he was going to strike. His heart beat a little faster when he suddenly lost sight of Phelan. Panicking, Eron slid behind a tall tree and curled up into a ball, holding a large stick across his knees. He shut his eyes and rocked back and forth.

Mina would never see him again.

Screams. Timo calling to him in those horrific screams.

I'm sorry. I'm so very sorry for not paying attention. For not understanding the world I live in. For not caring enough to learn from the past and be ready for the present. I'm so sorry, Mina. Please, please forgive me, he thought as he waited for imminent death.

Then, someone grabbed hold of his shoulders and shook him. When he opened his eyes, Phelan's blue face was just centimeters away from his own.

"Hey, where'd you go? You all right?" Eron asked.

"I scouted ahead. There's three of them, all light-skinned like you. If I had to guess, they're from your colony or maybe Cape Rouge. I heard them talking, not about much really. I did hear one call the other Laird. His name, I guess."

Eron uncurled himself and tried to stand. His weak ankle made it a struggle.

"Laird? Are you sure?" he asked. His knuckles turned white as he clenched the stick, scanning the forest for the boys.

"Yeah, why?" Phelan said.

"I've met them. Sort of. They were hunting a boy I knew named Bello. Did they say anything about Bello?"

"Not that I heard. All they talked about was finding food. Who's Bello?" Phelan said.

"Someone I knew once. I hope they didn't hurt him."

"Was he a friend of yours?"

"No, he liked to pick on me. Called me a coward. I hated him."

"Then why are you worried if they caught him? Seems like it would benefit you if they did."

"I don't want to see anyone get hurt. As much as I hated him, he is still a guy like me. He doesn't deserve to die."

Phelan peered at Eron and let the subject drop.

"Well, they're not too far away. They've stopped for now. If they catch us, be ready for a fight. They won't hesitate to kill us. You need to be ready for that. I'm trusting you, Eron."

Eron nodded, hoping they boys never discovered them.

Twenty-One

Eron and Phelan tracked the boys for most of the day. Late in the afternoon, they stopped to drink from a stream and lost sight of them.

"Eron, did you see where they went?" Phelan said.

"No. I thought you had your eyes on them. I stooped to get a drink and then they were gone."

Phelan slammed his fists against his legs. "They can't be too far away. Come on, we need to find them."

Phelan stormed off with Eron not too far behind. They ignored cover and walked in the open, frantically searching for the three boys.

"Slow down, Phelan. You know it's hard for me to keep up," Eron said. The other boy turned back.

"Come on! We're gonna lose them, if we haven't already. We have to stay close. We don't need them surprising us," Phelan said.

Overhead, gracers chattered away as they flew through the trees. Eron looked up, mesmerized by their elaborate and graceful motions. They went faster and faster every which way, as though they didn't care where they were going.

When Eron turned his attention back to the forest and their search for the boys, he and Phelan were standing in a clearing. Trees loomed overheard, creating a vibrant red and orange canopy, but there was no brush around the trunks. Either it just didn't grow there, or had been cleared away. It was a great place, and under different circumstances, he could see building a fort or having a secret place to meet someone... Mina, maybe? But with danger all around, it felt too exposed.

"Phelan, have you seen them? I don't like this."

Phelan shook his head. "No. I think we're on the right path, though. From the looks of the underbrush, someone's been through here recently."

"What underbrush?" Eron said, sweeping his arms at the lack of it.

"Before now, I mean. I've been following it until we got here. The trail continues over there," Phelan said, pointing to the far side of the clearing.

They started for the path, and a few steps later, Eron fell into a large hole camouflaged with branches and leaves. He let go of his stick as he stumbled, and it crashed down on his head.

"Ouch!" he yelled. Phelan ran to the edge of the pit and peered down.

"Eron! You all right down there?" he said.

Eron lay at the bottom, his arms and legs splayed.

"I think so," he said, coughing. A bolt of pain shot through his ribs and he winced. "Ow. Maybe not," he said.

"Stay put. I'll get something to help you out of there." Phelan's head disappeared.

Eron lay on his back, red dirt covering his shirt. He moaned in pain and held his ribs. It felt like someone had stabbed him with a hot knife and twisted. Each inhale brought new waves of pain.

A scratching sound caught his attention and he forgot about the pain. He turned toward the noise and noticed steps dug into the dirt, leading down into the black of a deeper cave below. He hadn't noticed it earlier, but now with his eyes adjusting to the dark, he could see his surroundings. There were also steps around the walls going up and out of the pit. Eron figured Phelan must not have seen them.

"Phelan," he said in a weak voice. It hurt to call out. "Phelan, there are steps." His voice didn't carry and he didn't have the strength or ability to ignore the pain in his ribs to yell for him.

Again, he heard a noise from within the cave. He was chilled by a draft.

"Phelan, hurry! I think something's in here!" he said. The walls of the pit swallowed his voice.

Coming from the black hole, he heard what sounded like hundreds of tiny clawed feet scratching at the dirt. Eron shivered. "Phelan, please hurry!" he called out louder, ignoring the pain in his side.

"Hey Eron, you still down there?" Phelan said, startling him. Eron looked up at the grinning blue face peering over the edge of the pit.

"Hurry up! There's something down here. Steps, along the side," Eron said, pointing to the indented wall below Phelan. He was standing at the bottom of the pit now. He couldn't get out by himself. He needed Phelan's help up the treacherous steps. Backing away from the cave, Eron made his way to the opposite side of the pit as Phelan carefully climbed down the steps.

He wiped his hands on his pants. "Whew, that was tough. I don't know how we're going to get you out—" he said and stopped when he caught sight of Eron staring into the blackness on the other side of the pit.

"What?" he said. Eron pointed.

"Something's down there," he said. His body trembled. Little red pebbles fell down the walls of the pit where Phelan had climbed down.

"Are you sure?" He crept closer to the opening and listened. "I hear it! Do you think you can get out of here? I'd rather not see what's making that noise."

"I can try," Eron said. Grabbing hold of one of the footholds in the wall, Eron tried to pull himself up. Searing pain shot through his chest and he let go, falling to the ground.

"Ow! No, I don't think I can make it," he said, rubbing his elbow. Phelan looked toward the cave.

"In there?" he said.

"No! There's got to be another way!" Eron said.

Above them, they heard twigs snapping.

"Hey, what's over there? Kumo, do you see that hole?" a voice above the pit said.

"Oh no!" Eron said, "it's those guys!"

"Eron, we only have one choice. The cave. They'll kill us if they find us."

Eron turned back toward the cave. The scratching started again, making his skin crawl

"Ok, let's go," Eron said. Phelan led the way down the steps and into the cave.

Twenty-Two

A dank, musty smell greeted the boys as they descended into the cave. As they moved farther in, the darkness swallowed them like a craate devouring a gracer. The light grew dimmer and dimmer, the scratching grew louder and closer. Behind them, they heard the boys talking.

"Wow, look at that, Steen! It's a pit. What do you think it was that fell in? I don't see anything," Laird said.

"Maybe we should check it out. See any way down?" It was Laird again.

Eron turned towards Phelan, his face hardly recognizable in the darkness. "Think they'll see the steps?"

"I doubt it. I didn't see them until you pointed them out, and my eyes are much better than yours," Phelan said.

"How do you know they are?" Eron said. Phelan grabbed his arm, hurrying him down the last few steps.

"Come on, before they do something stupid," Phelan said. Eron was lost in the darkness. He had no idea how big or small the cave was. The scratching was much clearer than before, though it didn't sound any closer.

"Go this way," Phelan said, directing Eron's arm. The boy stumbled, unsure where to place his next step.

"Hurry. Just keep going. There's nothing in our way."

"How do you know? I can't see a thing!"

"I told you, my eyes are better than yours. I wasn't just bragging. My people have enhanced vision. A perk of being blue, I guess. I can see for several meters in pitch black just like it was daylight. I can't see what's making that noise, though, and that worries me. Now, come on. It goes this way." Phelan led them deeper into the cave. The voices of the boys faded the farther they went.

"Maybe we can just wait here until they're gone," Eron said.

"We can, but whatever is making that sound isn't going away. I'd rather not wait for whatever it is to attack us."

Eron shuffled his feet, then followed Phelan.

The scratching quickened.

"What is that?" Eron said.

"I see it now! Oh, no! Hurry, Eron! Run!" Phelan said. He grabbed Eron's arm and pulled him forward.

The boys ran in darkness. Because of his enhanced vision, Phelan avoided protrusions from the walls, but Eron smacked into roots and other formations repeatedly, slowing their progress. Behind them, the scratching became more furious.

"I can't keep up," Eron said.

"Yes, you can. You have to. They're getting closer!"

Eron slowed to a walk. Ankle, ribs, and his legs were all burning. "I need to stop. I can't run anymore."

Phelan ran back to Eron, urging him forward. "Come on, you can do this. I think there's a way out up ahead."

"I can't! I'm too tired. My body hurts all over."

"Would you rather be dead? Get moving!" Phelan said.

Eron's body cried in pain with every movement.

"Phelan, can't we just wait? I don't think those guys are coming down here."

"Eron, quit stalling! We have to move, or did you forget about that thing? "

Phelan took a few steps towards the back of the cave, but Eron wouldn't budge.

"I'm done. I'm not going. You can go ahead, but I'm staying put."

The scratching became deafening.

"Eron, look out!" Phelan said. A long creature with sharp mandibles and twenty short legs on each side lunged at the boy. Its pincers caught one of his legs and squeezed, slicing through his pants and his flesh with ease.

A second creature joined the first and Eron was caught in a tug of war.

Eron screamed as the creatures tore into him. If the boys were anywhere near the pit, they'd have heard him for sure. Phelan lunged at the attackers.

He stabbed the first one, piercing its tough shell and plunging his knife into the soft muscle underneath. The deafening shriek reverberated throughout the cave. Eron kicked out, knocking it into the wall. It smacked against it and slid down, its feet still scratching the dirt beneath it. Phelan slammed his knife hard into its back. Its feet shot straight out as its life was extinguished.

The other one nipped at Phelan after releasing

Eron's leg. It hissed and clawed at him. Phelan jumped to the side as it struck. He veered to the other side when it lunged again, but the creature seemed to anticipate the move and caught his leg. Eron beat it with his fists. He kicked, but it only served to anger the beast. It hissed louder while clamping down harder on Phelan's leg.

"Get it off me! Get it off me!" Phelan said. "If its saliva mixes with my blood, it'll kill me!" Phelan struggled against its hold. He swung his knife down and missed. Frantic, Eron kicked harder, pain shooting through him. His ankle screamed in protest. He pushed through and caught the soft belly of the creature with his foot. It released Phelan as it tumbled across the cave floor.

"There!" Phelan said, pointing at it, but Eron couldn't make it out. Lunging forward, Eron struck blindly with his knife.

Silence filled the cave. The thing was dead.

Eron's heart beat fast and he heard Phelan breathing heavy.

"Eron, if those guys are out there, they surely heard this. We need to move. Now." Phelan removed the knife from the creature and wiped its blood on his pants. The blood smear glowed faintly.

"Their blood glows for a while. It's kind of neat, but deadly if it mixes with ours. Just don't get it in a cut or in your mouth. Bad things happen," Phelan said.

Eron exhaled. "Good to know."

"They really didn't teach you anything in Rippon, did they? I'm surprised you're still alive out here. Come on, I think I saw light this way." Phelan led them deeper into the cave where it grew darker before a pinpoint of light finally appeared far ahead. As they approached, Eron saw bright yellow leaves and sunlight. They'd found an escape.

CHAPTER

Twenty-Three

The boys collapsed in exhaustion when they finally emerged from the cave. It was late afternoon and the sun was making its slow path towards the horizon. They lay on their backs, looking up at the shadows created by the large trees overhead. An occasional animal flew by. Something scurried across the forest, but neither boy moved. After what they'd encountered, it didn't seem like something to worry about.

"What the heck were those things?" Eron asked. The other boy giggled.

"Those were dirt grubbers. They have a scientific name, but we've always just called them dirt grubbers. They're aggressive if threatened. We must've fallen into their nest."

"But someone made that pit. There were steps in the side and going down into the cave," Eron said.

"Hmm, that's true. What it means for us is that we should be more aware of our surroundings. There are others out here that we haven't even seen," Phelan said.

The boys lay there for quite a while. Eron's adrenaline began to fade, and he felt every ache in his body. It hurt to move. It even hurt to think.

"Should we go to a safer place?" Eron asked.

Phelan turned his head, grimacing. "Like where? We're in as safe a place as we can be. If we keep an eye on the cave, we'll see any intruders. These trees will give us some protection. And if it rains, we can creep back into the cave. It didn't look like anyone had been here in a while. I think we'll be fine. Besides, I'm tired. And I'm sore."

"Yeah, me, too. Are you sure it's safe, though? What if more of those things, the dirt grubbers, come after us?" Eron said.

"I'm not too worried. They'd most likely be here by now. I think it's a chance we can take."

The boys finally forced themselves to get up and forage for something to eat. They found a few insects and leaves that were edible, though they tasted horrible.

They placed twigs and leaves around the area to alert them of intruders and spent the night huddled near the cave's entrance. When morning came alive with the bright red sun and animals hurrying about their business, Eron's body was weak and aching.

"Morning," Phelan said. He was eating a good-sized grub when Eron woke. "Here, want one?" he said, holding out a squirming purple thing toward him. It didn't look the least bit appetizing, but he took it anyway. Eron bit down on the wriggling grub and its blood squirted into his mouth. It was hot and tasted like dirt, but it was nutrition. Food was scarce and anything helped. He squeezed his eyes shut as he chewed the rest of it.

"Tasty, huh?" Phelan grinned. Blood ran down his blue chin, his white teeth stained purple.

"Something like that," Eron replied. They both laughed, which hurt Eron's side.

"You all right, there?" Phelan said, pointing at Eron's ribs.

"Yeah, I think so. It hurts bad. I hope I didn't break anything. I'm not sure how much more I can take."

Phelan turned his head slightly, looking over Eron. "We've got some catching up to do. Can't sit here all day. Time is short. Come on, let's go," Phelan said.

The boys cleaned the area to cover their tracks. Eron found another large stick to use as a staff, and off they went on their search for the boys. If they didn't find them, then at least they were headed in the right direction to finish.

Several times they thought they'd spotted the boys, but each turned out to be a false alarm. Once it was a tree stump; another time, a bush. They'd crept up close to a form that turned out to be one of the Forgotten; a shorter one. They quietly backed away, not wanting to startle it. They watched it for a while before it scampered off into the forest.

Eron moved well enough with the staff. His ankle was stiff at first, but it finally loosened and didn't send shocking bursts of pain through his leg. His ribs were another story. Twisting felt as if he was being stabbed by hundreds of tiny knives, which he discovered when he bent to pick up his staff. He cried out in pain. Phelan ran to him.

"What is it? Did someone attack you?" he said.

"No, just my ribs. It'll pass," Eron said. It took a moment before he could continue.

Just after noon, they heard familiar laughter in the forest somewhere ahead of them. They dropped to the ground and slowly raised up, wary of being spotted. Eron stifled a scream of pain, but it was masked by the mocking laughter.

"Stay here. I'll check it out," Phelan said.

Hiding behind a bush, he watched as the boys toyed with a smaller boy.

"Look at him! He's begging," said the red-haired boy.

"Yeah! What a wimp," said the taller blond boy.

"Laird, he's ready to die. Should we help him?" the red-haired boy said.

Kumo leaned against a staff, his foot wrapped in cloth. He egged on his friends. "Come on, give it to him, Steen! He's ready to die. Look at the little boy. He's not ready to be a man. He'll never make it as a man."

The red-haired boy, Steen, smacked the boy's mouth. His head jerked back, blood and spit spraying.

"That's right, boy," Laird said, "you aren't a man. You don't deserve to make it through the Selection. Your mommy should've taught you better. What's your name?"

"It's Connor. My name is Connor. I'm from Rippon. Please, don't hurt me. Don't kill me. I want to make it to the end." Kneeling before the three boys, Connor lowered his head and stretched his arms out. "I'm not a threat. I'll leave you guys be. Please, just let me go."

Laird punched Connor in the eye, sending his head lolling to the side. Kumo swung his staff, narrowly catching Connor's stomach. Steen kicked at the ground, dirt clinging to the sweat on Connor's face.

Phelan watched the boys, unaware that Eron had snuck up behind him.

"Are those—hey, it's Connor!" he said, startling

Phelan.

"Be quiet! They'll hear you," Phelan whispered.

"But I know him. That's Connor! He's from the colony. He's my friend. We've got to do something."

Phelan raised his hand to his forehead. "I don't know Eron, maybe we should leave them alone. We've got ourselves to worry about. Are you really able to do something? Are you willing to act?"

"We have to. He's my friend!"

Phelan paused. "All right, I think we can help."

Twenty-Four

"Listen, Eron, we've got to act fast. I can't have you wussing out on me. We may have to kill them. Can you do that?"

Connor cried out as the boys poked him and smacked him around.

"Yeah, I think I can," Eron said.

"No, you have to be sure. Once we make our move, there's no turning back."

"Please, don't hurt me! I'll help you. I'll do whatever you want," Connor said to the boys. The sound of his voice made Eron's heart drop. His friend was in trouble. He had to do something.

"Yes, I'm positive, Phelan. I'm ready. I have to help him."

"Ok, here's what we need to do. I'll get their attention so they leave him alone. When they get over here, swing your staff and hit them as hard as you can. Your ambush should distract them enough so I can attack with my knife. It might get bloody. Are you sure you can handle this?"

Eron closed his eyes and lowered his head. He'd never attacked anyone before.

"Please! Let me go. I won't do anything to you, I swear. I won't hurt you. I'll go back towards the colony if I have to. Please leave me alone," Connor begged.

"I can handle it, Phelan. Let's do this," Eron said.

Moving into position behind heavy cover, Eron clutched his staff with white knuckles. Phelan looked from him to the boys. With a deep breath, he stood.

"Hey. Let him go. There's three of you picking on someone much smaller. Why don't you come over here?" Phelan said.

"Who was that? Look, over there!" said the tall blond boy. Phelan stood waving his arms.

"Are you stupid? Or weak? Or both? I can take all of you on by myself. Look at you, messing with that boy. He's weak! Cowards." Phelan's face turned purple as he provoked them.

"I'll kill you myself! I don't need their help," Steen said, taking the bait. He raced towards Phelan, but they had not counted on only one of the boys coming after him. It was too late to change tactics.

Steen charged through the brush directly at Phelan. As soon as he passed Eron, he swung his staff. Steen screamed when it struck his back. Blow after blow rained down on him, Eron's anger fueling each swing. The sickening sound of bones crunching accompanied the loud smack of stick meeting flesh. Though his body hurt from the effort, Eron pushed through. Connor's life depended on it.

"Eron!" Connor yelled, recognizing his friend.

"Connor, we're here to help!"

Phelan took off towards the remaining two boys as did Eron, though moving much slower. Phelan raised his knife. "Now, it's my turn!" he said as he charged.

Laird smiled. Connor still on his knees in front of him, Laird calmly pulled a large black-handled knife from its sheath on his hip. Holding Connor's head with one hand, he slowly drew the knife across the boy's throat. Crimson blood flowed from his neck. Without a sound, Connor fell face down, staining the red ground a darker crimson.

"No!" Eron yelled. Laird grinned at him. Kumo laughed.

"Looks like you struck a nerve, Laird. And in that boy over there, too!" Both boys laughed.

Eron struggled through the thick brush. Phelan approached the boys and stopped, holding his knife in front of him defensively.

"You cowards! Fight me! Come at me!"

"Look, Kumo, a blue face. I always heard they were bad luck. You can't trust them. I bet he kills that other boy back there. If we let him live. Which we won't," Laird said.

Kumo and Laird flanked either side of Phelan. The boys poked at him, pushing him back.

"What's wrong, blue face? Scared? I thought you people were tougher than this. You're weaker than I expected. I wonder if your blood flows red like his," Laird said, pointing his knife at Connor.

"Why don't you shut up and find out?" Phelan said.

"I'd love to," Laird said. Taking a step to the side, then back towards Phelan, Laird lunged. Phelan jumped to the side and swung his knife, missing the boy. Kumo stumbled towards him and swung his staff, catching Phelan's leg and tripping him. Phelan landed and rolled out of the way before another strike came. Laird swung his knife from side to side, almost striking Kumo in the process.

"Hey, watch it, Laird! You almost got me!" Laird didn't reply. His face was frozen in a twisted sneer.

Before he could strike Phelan, Eron beat back Kumo with his own staff. Wood crashed on wood as Eron pushed him back. Laird continued to swing his blade, seeking a soft target.

"I'm gonna kill you all!" Laird said. "I fear no one!"

Phelan ducked the wild blade and swept Laird's legs out from under him. He fell to the side but rolled back to his feet.

"You'll need to do better than that, blue face!" Laird said. Phelan stood ready with his knife, waiting for the attack. But Laird remained still.

Kumo tried to flank Eron. He was forced to step near Connor, and he dropped his gaze for a moment. Kumo swung his staff, thumping him in the back. Eron fell on top of Connor, and he put his hands out to catch himself, covering them in his dead friend's blood. Rage grew hot inside him. Jumping up, he slammed the other boy with his staff and crunched his fingers. Kumo cried in pain as Eron swung his staff again like he'd done with Steen. Kumo backed away, but his injury made it difficult to get too far from Eron's furious swing.

The staff struck him in the face, the arms, his chest. Bones snapped and crunched. With all his rage behind it, Eron swung hard toward Kumo's head. A loud pop sounded and Kumo's eyes rolled back. He fell in a heap next to Connor.

The final blow snapped Laird out of his trance.

"Forget you, blue face! I'll get my revenge. I swear it!" Laird swung his blade, forcing Phelan back before running off into the forest.

Eron's staff was covered in blood.

"Connor," he said. "I'm so sorry." He dropped his staff and fell to his knees, crying.

Phelan inspected Kumo. "Turn away, Eron."

Phelan slid his knife in the base of Kumo's skull. The boy's body twitched, then stopped. Eron turned away as Phelan did the same to Steen.

Twenty-Five

"We have to bury him," Eron said. Blood stained the ground around Connor, his lifeless body face down in the crimson pool. "We can't just leave him like this. He was my friend. He deserves better."

Phelan was checking himself for wounds and looked out at the forest. "Don't think he'll come back anytime soon. If so, at least he's the only one left. We can take him by ourselves."

Dropping to a knee next to Connor, Eron wept.

"I should've done something for you. I'm so sorry this happened. I should've been there for you," he said. Phelan moved to his side and put his arm around Eron's shoulder.

"It's all right, Eron. It was quick. Maybe he didn't have any pain. At least he doesn't have to deal with those idiots ever again."

Phelan let Eron grieve, leaving him to be with the body. When he had composed himself, Eron approached his new friend.

"Can we bury him now?"

"I've been thinking about that. We don't have anything to dig with but we can cover him."

Eron closed his eyes. "It'll have to do."

The boys set out to gather rocks. It took some time, but they found enough to cover the body. They arranged the body and placed the stones on top. Eron squeezed Connor's hand one last time as they covered him.

When they were finished, the boys stood a distance away. A tear rolled down Eron's cheek. "Goodbye, Connor. I'll never forget you." They rested nearby, Eron staring at the pile of stones in silence.

Though in Eron's mind, it was anything but silent.

It started soon after they covered him. Screams. Timo's screams. They were back and louder than ever. Eron wanted to tear at his skull to get the awful noise to stop. Soon, Mina's voice called to him, blocking the screams. Asking him if he was going to make it. Asking if he was ready to cross over and be a man. His mother's voice followed. She cried. She begged forgiveness for not training him properly for the Selection and apologized. And then, Connor's voice. He called out to Eron, accusing him of not being there to help. His voice had an unusual tinge of anger. Eron felt horrible as he listened to Connor's accusations, knowing he couldn't have done anything for him.

Then his mind turned on him. *What if we'd have taken the boys back at the cave? What if I attacked them earlier after Bello brought them towards me? I could've done something then. Connor would still be alive. His death is on me. I let them live. My unwillingness to do what needed to be done is what killed him. I can't be weak again. I won't be weak. I caused his death.*

By the time the sun rose, Eron made up his mind to never be weak again. Strength was the only thing to carry a boy into manhood. He expected to beat the Selection and to do so, he'd need to be strong. Weakness brought only death.

"Phelan, we need to go," Eron said after daybreak. "I can't stay here any longer. We need to get to the end. I'm done with this."

Phelan nodded.

The boys travelled south to where the promise of a long and wonderful life waited for them. Eron wanted nothing more than to hold Mina in his arms and never let go. He'd be strong for her.

For the next several days, the boys marched in relative quiet. Eron had no desire to speak and Phelan seemed to sense there was no use in trying to get him to open up. It was a welcome change for Eron not having Phelan constantly badger him with questions or small talk. Unless Phelan asked if he needed a break, not a word was spoken between the two. When they reached a large clearing in the forest where only tall grass grew, Phelan spoke up.

"Hey, Eron, I know it's been tough on you. The Selection has always been about separating the boys from the men in a very real and cruel way.   Fortunately for you, you're still here. You have a chance at an idyllic new life if we make it to the end. We're closer now. We have ten days left. This is the halfway point. We're that close! If we can just be careful, we'll have an easy second leg of the journey. Except for in the valley, but we'll see how bad it is when we get there."

Eron turned to face him.

"Connor deserved to see his way to the other side. What makes us different than him? Why do we get to continue? This entire process is messed up. Don't you think so, too? Who makes boys go through horrors like this, just to prove our worth as men? It's insane!

None of it makes sense. Hasn't anyone ever questioned it?"

"Rippon must be an odd place. We're taught the validity of the Selection at an early age. None of it seems odd. It's the way it is, because it has to be. Don't you understand?"

"No! Not at all. We weren't taught any of the reasons why the Selection makes sense. None!"

"Are you sure about that? You also said your colony had no name, but I clearly heard your friend mention Rippon before..." he paused. "Before he was killed."

Eron thought back to the events of Connor's death. He'd been over them a hundred times or more looking for ways he could've saved him.

"Yeah, he did say it," he said quietly. Phelan stared at him.

"Then, are you sure you weren't taught all this stuff and forgot, or did you stop paying attention? Maybe you got hit in the head and it caused you to forget. Maybe there was some other trauma that removed everything about the Selection from your mind."

Eron slammed his fists together. "I was not hit in the head! I know what I know, and the stupid Selection isn't part of it!"

"All right, then; calm down. I'm just trying to help. Hey, why don't we make camp here for the night? It'll be dark by the time we get past this clearing. We can start fresh tomorrow."

"Yeah, sure. I don't care."

Twenty-Six

When they started across the clearing the next morning, Eron's mood had changed considerably.

"Phelan, are we really that close?" Orangish stalks of thin grass waved back and forth, brushing their knees as they walked through the field.

"Yeah. We're just about halfway there. From what I understand, this last half is different than the first. By now most of the other boys in here have been..." he hesitated.

"Have been what?" Eron said.

"I don't want to sound insensitive, that's all."

"Go ahead, I'm fine. You were about to say most of the boys have been thinned out. They've been culled from the herd to make way for the stronger ones. Like us."

Phelan nodded. "Something like that. Sorry. I know it sounds harsh, especially after Connor."

"It is harsh. It has to be, right? That's the way of the Selection." His voice held a tinge of anger.

A black figure raced across the clearing.

"What was that?" Eron said. It was right in front of them before they saw it, and disappeared just as quickly. He'd grabbed his staff and held it up, ready to defend.

"I'm not sure. A Forgotten, maybe? I thought the clearing would give us a visual on anything trying to sneak up on us. Did you see where it came from or where it went?" Phelan said.

"It showed up out of nowhere, then vanished. We should go that way," Eron said pointing left, opposite from where the figure went.

About an hour later, another black figure streaked across the clearing in the same direction as the other had.

"Did you see that?" Eron said. Phelan nodded.

"Yeah. It's like the other one. Stay alert."

The boys were quiet as they continued on. Scanning the clearing for any other surprises, they'd made it across the waving grass. By midday, they neared the other side. The trees offered welcome shade from the hot red sun.

"Let's take a break here," Phelan said. There were berry bushes near the tree line. "We can eat these. They'll help us until we can find something more substantial."

They picked almost all the berries off the bushes and devoured them with abandon. Bright yellow juice dripped down their chins.

"Compared to grubs, these are spectacular!" Eron said. The berries were sour with a hint of sweetness. Phelan grinned, his teeth stained yellow from the juice.

"They are pretty special. I haven't had any in a long time," Phelan said.

As the boys gorged themselves, another black figure darted ahead of them in the forest. Eron almost choked on his mouthful of berries.

"Phelan! Over there! I saw it again!" he said pointing into the forest.

"The Forgotten? In there?" Phelan said. He'd been crushing the berries in his hands and licking the juice off his fingers.

"Yes! I think we're being watched."

Phelan cleaned his fingers and stared at the forest. "I don't see anything."

"It was going that way," Eron said pointing out a path with his green-stained hands.

"Do you think it's following us?" Phelan said.

"I guess it's possible. Do you think it was the one we fought off before?" Eron said.

"I doubt it. There's bound to be more of them out here. Keep your eyes open. We don't want to get caught off guard."

Eron finished the last of his berries, scanning the area for any sign of the creature. For several minutes, he paused, looking out into the forest, but nothing appeared.

"Let's be careful how we proceed. There might be something waiting for us," Eron said.

Twenty-Seven

"Who do you think made this path? Do you think anyone is still here?" Eron said as they walked.

"Who knows. The Selection's been going on for decades. Longer even. This could've been here from the beginning. It doesn't really matter, I guess. So long as we're careful, we should be fine," Phelan said.

"I suppose so. Still, don't you ever wonder how things came to be? Why certain things are the way they are?"

"Eron, it's your own fault you know nothing about the Selection. I'm positive they trained you in Rippon. I mean, what parent would send their son here without preparation? For some reason, you forgot. Not your finest moment, but that's only my guess. Maybe they didn't prep you; maybe they did. It doesn't really matter anymore. You're here and alive. That's what matters. You can make it if you want to. We both can."

"I feel like I'm missing something. Like I should know all this. But you're right. We can make this together," Eron said.

The boys continued deeper into the forest. The early evening rays of red sun grew dimmer as they went farther in. Shadows danced around them. The often-noisy animals were settling in for the night. Ahead, the trees thinned out, indicating another clearing. As they got closer, they saw it wasn't a normal break in the trees.

"I was wondering when we'd come across this," Phelan said. Beyond the forest's edge, they stood on a cliff overlooking a canyon. As far as Eron could see in both directions was a sheer rock ledge.

"Now what?" he said to Phelan.

"We go down. There's a path to the valley cut into the cliffs. We've just got to find it."

"How do you know all this stuff? Wait. Don't tell me. I should've learned all this in school. Never mind," Eron said.

"Actually, I heard about it from some of the few old timers in Greater Manthus."

Eron shrugged. "Ok, so where do we start?"

Phelan walked closer to the cliff's edge, looking both ways. "Let's try that way," he said, pointing to the right.

The boys edged along the cliff. Sheer red rock faces lined their side of the valley. The far end of the valley was obscured by cover of heavy trees and low yellow clouds.

"Looks like storms moving in," Eron said, pointing at the clouds.

"Good thing we're above them, isn't it? Let's make camp up ahead, and in the morning, we'll look for the way down." Several meters along the cliff's edge, they built a crude shelter and foraged for food. They found a few grubs and edible grass. It would have to do.

"I can't wait until we get out of here and get some real food," Eron said. They were leaning against the small rock wall that formed the backside of their camp and looking over the canyon and valley below. The sun was sinking below the horizon and stars shined brightly in the sky above. The moon was just peeking above the trees.

"I can taste it now. A nice juicy buff steak. Medium rare, with a side of mashed roots," Phelan said. Eron's stomach rumbled.

"That sounds fantastic!"

They sat in silence for a while before Eron spoke.

"Phelan, after we get out of here, will we ever see each other again? I mean, will you go back to your colony and that's it?"

"I'm not sure. I suppose I will. After I get my bride, of course!" he said, punching the other boy on the arm.

"Ha, yeah I guess there's that, too. I'll be so busy with her, that I'll forget all about you!" Eron said. He returned the punch.

They laughed and quieted down again.

"Well, what will happen? Is this it? What do we do with our lives after we make it through the Selection?"

"We live in bliss! We get a wife, we settle down, we have children, and we live a long life until we die at an old age. At least, that's my plan," Phelan said.

"If that's true, why didn't I know much about my dad? Why wasn't he around? I have an older sister and brother, but I don't know much about my dad at all. Do you? About your dad, I mean."

Phelan looked down and tossed a stick off the cliff.

"No, not really. After I was born, he went to the Defense Force. That's what my mom said, anyway."

"Mine, too," Eron said. "Is that the life we get when this is all done? Is this just preparation for that? Are we in some ridiculous boot camp and whoever makes it through gets the privilege of joining the military?"

Eron said.

"You do ask a lot of questions, you know that?"

"I like to know things. Don't you?"

"There you go with the questions again!" Phelan said.

"Sorry, I'll stop." He laughed a little and Phelan nodded.

"I hope we find something good down there. I could use a break from all this fighting," Phelan said.

"I agree. Maybe we'll find some buffs roaming around and get us a thick steak now!"

They fell silent again, staring up at the night sky. The moon cast a pinkish glow on the yellow clouds below in the valley. Stars grew brighter.

"I do hope this will be easier now," Eron said breaking the silence. "I'm done with hurting people."

"If we aren't, at least you know you can do it," Phelan said.

It took a while, but eventually they rested.

Twenty-Eight

It took most of the next morning, but they found the path leading down the cliff face. They'd passed it several times before Eron spotted the first step.

The ledge was only half a meter wide and the path was treacherous. Winds whipped at them as they clung to the cliff, hoping to avoid being caught up in a gust and knocked to the valley below.

"Phelan, are you sure there's no other way?" Eron said. Both boys were pressed flat against the red rock and moving slowly along the narrow path.

"Positive. It's the only way, and one of the last great obstacles. Many have died here."

"I can understand why," Eron said. A foothold loosened, sending pebbles and rocks tumbling down the cliff. Eron pulled his foot back fast and almost lost his balance. His knuckles went white as he clung to what little purchase he had in the rocks.

"Careful now; it wouldn't be good to lose your balance up here," Phelan said.

Overhead, large yellow-headed anthels swirled in the windy sky. The translucent membrane of their large brown wings stretched wide to catch the current and drift along. Typically, they ate other animals, preferring live ones, though they were known to feast on carcasses. Alive or dead, the boys were desperately trying not to be a meal.

They descended about a third of the way down the cliff face along the dangerous path. A wide landing greeted them and they stopped to rest.

As they sat there, Phelan cupped his eyes and scanned the valley. "It's beautiful down there, don't you think?"

Eron looked down. "Yeah, I guess."

"Have you ever seen anything like this? Being up so high and having this view? It's spectacular."

"If you say so. To me, it looks dangerous. It looks like a trap."

"Why would you think that?"

"I don't know. It just does. I feel like we're heading to a battle we aren't prepared for. And down there, those trees and the colors and everything is just a trap."

"So why go down here with me?" Phelan said. His eyes narrowed as he looked at Eron.

"What else am I going to do? You said there was no other way. Unless you lied, but I don't think you did. I hope not, anyway. I don't want to die. Not up here. Not down there. I want to make it to the end. I want to see Mina again. I want to live."

Phelan grinned. "Of course, you want to live! We all do! We'll make it, Eron, you'll see. We'll be jumping up and down, crying and laughing when we see Victory Point. And I'm sure this girl of yours will be waiting with open arms to give you a big, fat, wet kiss!"

Eron's face turned bright red. "I hope so!" he said.

"Here, want some berries?" Phelan said. He'd saved some from earlier. Though they stained his pocket, they were still edible. Eron reached out to get a few and the rocks shifted beneath him.

He slid toward the edge. The loose gravel made it difficult to grab on to anything. His legs swung over the edge, kicking rocks down the cliff. He scrambled and tried to push his way back up with his feet, but he slid on pebbles and dirt.

Phelan tossed the berries and lunged toward Eron, grabbing his arms. Heaving and straining, he pulled and stopped the downward momentum.

"Come on, Eron, push yourself up! I can't hold you much longer," Phelan said. Spittle flew from his mouth. Veins pulsed on his blue forehead.

"I'm trying! I can't brace my feet on anything. Help me, Phelan!"

The other boy pulled harder as he tried to heave Eron over the ledge. His feet slipped and he almost went over, sending them both down. At the last moment, a large rock gave him something to support against and stop the momentum. Using the leverage, he pulled back and tried to bring Eron up the ledge before he lost his strength.

"Come on, Eron, my arms are giving out. I can't hold this!" Phelan said.

Eron looked down into the valley. "Just let me go. I'm not gonna make it. Don't waste your time, Phelan. I'm not strong enough for this. You are. Let me go."

"No! Don't give up. We're so close now! Push yourself up now, or I go with you over the edge."

"That's stupid, Phelan! If you let me go, at least you'll have a chance."

"I said no! It's both of us, or neither of us. Call it, Eron."

Eron closed his eyes. Shifting his legs, his foot

bumped into something solid. He raised himself up a bit.

"That's it, Eron! Push!"

Then Phelan pulled as hard as he could with the little bit of help from Eron and it was enough to lift the boy back on the ledge.

Both boys sat against the cliff wall breathing heavy, sweat dripping down their faces.

"Thank you, Phelan. Thank you for not letting me go."

Phelan punched him in the arm. "Don't ever give up. Under any circumstances, don't you ever give up. Do you hear me? I might not always be able to help. You have to want to live, Eron."

"I got it. Sorry. I saw no other way."

"There's always a way if you want it bad enough. Next time, stay close to the wall. I don't think I can do that again."

By the time the sun had set, they'd made it down into the lush valley.

Twenty-Nine

Thin everpurple needles covered the valley floor. They were soft and quiet to walk on, quite the contrast to the forest. The boys made camp under one of the vibrant everpurple trees. They slept soundly that night, better than any night yet.

When they awoke and continued their journey, the mood was upbeat and expectant.

Larger gracers flew overhead. They were at least five times the size of their cousins on higher ground. Large oval-shaped leaves on thick stems burst forth from shrubs like Eron had never seen before. The green leaves had small white pods on the undersides.

"Stay away from those spores," Phelan said. "You get them on your skin, and they'll burn right in. You can't wash them off. There's a salve made of concentrated spearleaf and broadwind seed oil that clears them from your skin, but...we don't have any. It's best to stay away."

Eron stepped back from the leaves. "Ok, then," he said.

A rock landed on the ground in front of them. Eron looked to Phelan, who shrugged. Another one rolled next to Eron's foot. The rocks were coming from behind them. Turning around, they saw a boy standing twenty meters away.

"Hey, coward. I thought I'd catch up with you.

Who's that? You need someone to fight for you?"

Bello. He was a bit thinner and his eyes were sunken in his skull.

"Oh no," said Eron. He gripped his staff tight.

"Who's that?" Phelan asked.

"That's the guy from my colony that messed with me. His name is Bello. He's a jerk."

"And alone," said Phelan. "What do you want?" Phelan said to the larger boy.

Bello smirked. "So, you do need his help, huh, coward? I knew you'd never make it alone. Just like your brother."

Eron slammed his staff on the ground with shaking arms. His lips were tight.

"He's with me. Anyone has a problem with Eron has a problem with me," Phelan said.

"Shut up, blue face. Your kind are liars and cowards, just like him. I'm not afraid of you. Don't get in my way." Bello stood with his hands balled into fists at his sides. He tapped them on his legs.

"You know," Phelan said to Eron, "I'm getting a bit tired of being called blue face. What's that supposed to mean, anyway? Of course, my face is blue! All my skin is. Idiots."

"If all you've got is blue face, then you might be the one to worry," Phelan said. Bello's eyes narrowed. Startled by a sound in the bush near him, Bello jumped to the side. Eron laughed at the comical way he moved.

"Shut up!" Bello yelled. He ran towards the two boys, smashing through bushes and branches. Phelan and Eron took defensive stances as the larger boy came at them.

Suddenly, Laird sprung from a bush and slammed into Bello, knocking him to the ground. Eron and Phelan looked to each other, then watched as Laird pummeled Bello.

"I'm going to kill you!" he screamed. Bello held his hands over his face against the blows. Fists flew as Laird beat on the unsuspecting boy. Blood sprayed. Bello cried out.

"We've got to do something!" Eron said.

"Like what? It seems like he's taking care of your problem," Phelan said.

Ignoring Phelan, Eron rushed to the boys, raising his staff high. Laird looked up and smiled.

"You won't do it," he said, "because he's right. You're a coward."

Eron pulled back and swung his staff at Laird, knocking him in the head. Wood connected with flesh. A sickening snap sounded and Laird screamed. Eron swung again. And again. Laird tried to block the blows, but only made Eron angrier. He swung harder, snapping the boy's fingers. Laird's blood splattered on Eron when the staff smashed into his mouth, forcing him off Bello.

"Get off him!" Eron screamed. A large red spot tainted Laird's blond hair.

"I'm going to kill you!" he said to Eron through bloody lips.

"Not today," Eron said.

Laird left Bello on the ground and lunged at Eron. "I'm gonna enjoy killing you!" he shouted. Eron swatted at him with his staff, the blow barely registering on Laird. The taller boy caught Eron in the stomach, forcing him to the ground. He kneed Eron in the groin and the smaller boy yelled in pain.

The boys struggled on the ground, a tangle of arms and legs in a furious dance of death. Laird punched Eron in the ribs, striking harder with each hit.   Eron cringed in pain. "Phelan, help," he called. Laird backhanded him in the mouth, spit and blood spraying.

Bello lay on the ground moaning. Phelan remained still.

"You don't deserve to live!" Laird screamed. "You're weak!"

Eron struggled against the larger boy's grasp. He shifted and squirmed underneath, trying to free himself. Laird struck him in the stomach, winding him. Eron could barely see the boy on top of him, his vision turning hazy.

A rock struck Laird on the head. He let up on his punishment. "Ouch, what the—" he said. Eron didn't wait. He pushed upwards, knocking Laird off him. Phelan stood grinning, another rock in his hands.

"Kill him, Eron! Do it now, before he recovers!" Phelan said.

Eron forced himself up and grabbed his staff. He paused, then swung the staff down, striking Laird on the head. The boy's skull caved inward from the vicious hit. Blood streamed from his nose. His eyes rolled back in his head. Eron was poised to strike again as Laird lay splayed on the ground. Dead.

Bello stood on wobbly legs, screaming. "Why did you do that, coward? I can handle myself! I don't need help from someone like you! I never needed your help!" In a blind rage, Bello ran into the forest, screaming at the top of his lungs. "I don't need help from cowards! Leave me alone!"

Phelan watched the boys without moving. Eron released his grip on the staff. "Why didn't you help earlier?" he said to Phelan. The other boy raised his hand as if to stop Eron from talking.

"You had it under control."

Bello's voice disappeared in the valley and he was gone.

"What just happened?" Eron asked. His staff was covered in blood and Laird lay on the ground in a twisted heap.

"You survived. You saved someone who didn't deserve it," Phelan said.

"We all deserve a chance, Phelan. Did you know they were following us?"

"How would I know? I'm just as surprised as you were! They must've been following and waiting for a chance to strike. Seems like Bello didn't think it through. Neither did Laird. I had no idea you'd break like that. Not bad," he said.

Eron looked at his hands. "I, I didn't mean to kill him. I was only trying to get him off Bello."

"You did that," Phelan said. "We best keep an eye out for Bello. I don't think he appreciated the assistance."

"Yeah. Maybe he'll finally leave me alone."

He stood shaking, flexing his sore hands. "What have I done?" he said quietly. "What have I become?"

CHAPTER

Thirty

Eron wrestled with his emotions for quite a while after killing Laird. Would Timo have killed someone? he wondered. The pent-up rage that guided his staff when he swung it at the boy concerned him. He'd never felt so aggressive, so destructive before. He fought out of self-defense and helped beat Laird's crew, but this felt different to him.

"Phelan, do you ever get over killing someone?" he asked, his voice quiet and weak.

"What do you mean by that?" Phelan said.

Eron hesitated. "Nothing, I guess."

The boys had put some distance between them-selves and Laird's bloody body. They left it to the creatures of the forest. No doubt it had attracted craates and other animals looking to get a free meal. Eron shuddered at the thought of thousands of tiny insects already crawling, heaving, gorging themselves on the body.

Still, they had the problem of Bello to deal with. If they came across him again.

"Do you think you can kill Bello if it comes down to it? I mean, if you were in a situation where it was you or him and I wasn't there to help. Could you defend yourself and take his life if needed?" Phelan asked.

Eron stopped walking as Phelan continued, unaware he'd stopped. "It might come down to it. Think you got the guts to do it?" Turning, he noticed Eron wasn't right behind him.

"Hey, what are you doing back there?" Phelan said.

"I don't know. About Bello, that is. I just don't know. I don't want to kill him, but if my survival depends on his death, could I do it? There's no way he'd kill me, right? I've known him forever."

Phelan approached Eron, nudging his arm, and the boys continued forward.

"I see the ability to kill in his eyes. The way he looks at you, Eron, I'd be afraid. He's got a grudge against you, and I don't think he'd hesitate to kill you. For your own sake, I hope you're able to defend yourself and do what you need to do. I would if I were you."

"That's easy for you to say, Phelan. You've killed before. You were trained to defend yourself. I wasn't. Well, not that I remember, anyway."

"That's what gets me, Eron. I find it impossible to believe you weren't prepared for the Selection. It's the duty of every colony, e-v-e-r-y colony, to get their boys ready. I mean, how could they hope to gain thriving males if they don't tell you anything about it? I truly wonder if something happened to you to make you forget all about it. Something traumatic."

"Are you serious? I think I'd remember something as important as the Selection. I'm pretty damn sure I'd remember all the scenarios that could happen out here and the measures I'd have to take to survive. That kind of intense training and teaching is not something I'd forget. It's impossible!"

Phelan squinted at him. "Not impossible. Improbable, sure, but not impossible. I can't believe you guys in Rippon are so backwards that you'd not teach your boys the truth. You don't even remember the name of your colony or that there are other colonies on the planet." He dropped his head. "Connor remembered."

Eron shut his eyes tight. "Don't you dare use my friend against me. I can't explain that. Don't bring him up again."

"Sorry, but I think you're either lying to me, or something's wrong with your brain."

"Shut up, Phelan. I'm done talking about it. Drop it, ok?"

"Fine. But when the time comes, I might not be able to help if Bello attacks. And if I do attack, I won't hesitate to kill him. It's all about survival out here. By any means necessary. I hope you're ready."

Eron didn't reply. He kept walking, pushing his way through the brush.

———

"I'm going to kill you, coward!"

Eron's eyes bulged. Swinging his staff forward, he held it in front of him.

"Was that—" Phelan started.

"Bello," Eron said. "It's him. He's out there somewhere. Where do you think he is?" Cocking his head, he tried to pinpoint the direction of the voice.

"I'm going to kill you and blue face. Cowards don't deserve to live. And blue faces that help them don't, either."

Phelan turned to the left. "Over there, maybe? I don't know for sure. The sounds carry in a strange way down in this valley."

"Come on, coward, what are you going to do? You can't stop me! Blue face can't stop me. I'm going to kill you."

"Show yourself, Bello!" Eron said. "We can talk. We don't have to kill each other. We can help each other. We both want to live, right? Phelan and I can help you survive, and we can all make it out of here alive."

A noise came from the bushes fifteen meters away to the right. Phelan put his finger to his lips. Slowly he made his way towards the sound, staying low to avoid Bello catching him. As he approached the bush, he charged with his knife. A small, furry, bright green harmit hopped away chittering, its long ears standing straight in the air in anger.

Phelan looked back to Eron and shrugged.

"Stupid blue face has no idea where I am!" Bello said. The voice sounded like it was in front of them. Both boys scanned the forest, but saw nothing.

"Come on, Bello, we can work together. We've not always been friends, but we're equals out here. I can help you. We can help each other," Eron said.

From behind them, Bello replied, "I don't need help from cowards! You and blue face will never make it to the end. You both deserve to die. You're weak. I'll kill you both because I'm not weak. You're going to die!"

The boys jumped at the voice behind them. They crouched, preparing for an attack, but still nothing.

"Why's he doing this?" Phelan asked Eron. "Where is he? I can't tell."

"I don't know, Phelan. He's always had it out for me. He could be anywhere. This valley makes it impossible to locate the direction of his voice."

"Cowards! Look at you. It's as though you think you can stop me! You will both die by my bare hands, I swear it. I'm going to enjoy killing you, Eron! Blue face will just be a bonus."

To their left, they heard footsteps running away.

"Come on, then, let's stop talking and get to it!" Phelan said.

Silence.

"Who's the coward now?" Phelan called out.

For several moments, the boys waited for an answer and none came.

"I think he left," Eron said.

Phelan nodded. "Yeah, for now. We have to watch our backs. He'll be back, and you have to be ready. I don't think he's playing around. This is real, Eron. This is survival. I think we'll need to fight him and kill him before we get to the end. It's time to see what you're really capable of."

Thirty-One

There were only seven days left in the Selection. Eron and Phelan had gone three days since they'd last heard Bello. At first, Eron could barely sleep at night. Every sound woke him, expecting it to be Bello's attack. By the third night he slept through most of the sounds, though some of the louder ones frightened him from his slumber. The boys made it to the other side of the valley, and before them rose an imposing red cliff.

"This is it, Eron. Once we scale this, we're almost done. The edge of the forest is just over this cliff. I can almost feel the warm bed waiting for me!"

Eron looked up the intimidating cliff. The top disappeared into the yellow clouds. "Up there, huh?" he said.

"Yep. Once we find the path, it's up, up, up until there's no more up to go."

"Once we find the path? You don't know where it is?" Eron said.

"No. I've never been here, but unlike you, I remembered my lessons. There's a path that winds its way toward the top. It's supposed to be the hardest part of the entire Selection. Well, other than dealing with boys that want to kill you. Many have gotten this far, only to die from a nasty fall."

"Do you think Bello is up there?" Eron said. He scanned the cliff as far as he could see.

"If he got here ahead of us, he has to be. If he did, he has the advantage over us. We'd better be on guard."

"Understood," Eron said.

"Before we scale it, we might need to find some food for the trip. Let's look for berries or anything else we can find."

The boys split up and scavenged for food. When Eron started back to meet up with Phelan, something moved ahead of him. A black figure raced across the valley. Eron tensed.

"Phelan," he called out. Again, the figure raced ahead of him. It was closer this time.

"Phelan!" he said, "is that you?" Eron's knuckles clicked when he gripped his staff. He was anxious and hyper-sensitive. Every little sound or movement caught his attention. Leaves moving in the breeze made him jump. Gracers flying overhead almost made his heart burst from his chest.

The black figure ran in front of him, but a bit farther away, heading in the opposite direction as it had gone before.

"Phelan, this isn't funny," Eron said.

"What isn't?"

Eron's bladder nearly released. Phelan's voice was directly behind him. He hadn't heard him approach while he was engrossed in watching the black figure.

"Don't do that! You almost gave me a heart attack!" Eron said, holding a hand against his chest while trying to slow down his breathing.

"How did you sneak up on me like that? I could hear everything around me."

"Practice," Phelan said.

"Did you see that?" Eron said. He pointed to where the figure was moving back and forth.

"See what? The trees? The thick brush? The impossibly difficult rock wall we have to climb? I saw that."

"There was a black figure running ahead of me. Up that way." Again, pointing to where he last saw the thing moving. "I thought it was you. Maybe it's Bello or another Forgotten?"

"Are you sure about that? I was over there until I heard you making noise. I didn't see anything." He held a hand above his eyes and searched the area for any sign of the mysterious figure, but saw nothing. "Well, if there was something it's either hiding or gone, which is what we need to be. I'd like to get this last part over with before you back out on me," he said, nudging Eron.

"Come on, you really think I'd back out? I want out of here. I'm done with this stupid Selection. All I want to do is leave and hopefully find Mina waiting for me."

"That's what I want to hear! The food we have will need to do. Maybe we'll find something else along the way, though it doesn't look promising. There's hardly any vegetation up the rocks; maybe at the top, but I can't see because of the clouds. Ready?"

Eron took a last look around the area, hoping to catch sight of the figure. He felt as though someone was watching them. It unsettled him. There was nothing he could do about it now, unless they spent their quickly-dwindling time searching for it instead of finishing their journey.

"Yeah, let's find this path, Phelan. I'm ready."

The boys had trivial conversation that Eron tuned

out. Phelan seemed not to notice; he was content talking and practically answering himself. After a few hours, they found the path leading up the cliff face, closer to their destination. And Mina.

Thirty-Two

The first few meters of the climb were easy. Before long the boys were about a third of the way up without much effort.

"I thought you said this was the hardest part of the Selection, Phelan? Seems like someone lied to you."

"I wouldn't get too confident yet. We've got a long way to go before we can relax."

Eron paused. The thin outcrop of rock they were scaling felt secure under his feet. There was barely enough room to move on it, but it was a consistent width and free of obstacles. Looking back out over the valley, Eron admired the lush beauty of the forest. The other cliff they'd climbed down was on the far side of the valley. He scanned to the top and guessed where it was they'd descended. Laird's body lay down in the valley, hopefully already devoured by insects and other animals so no one came upon it. And maybe Bello was down there as well.

Eron watched as gracers flew across the treetops and waited to see if the black figure was down there. He wasn't sure what it was. It had to be Bello or one of the Forgotten. If they were lucky, it would still be down there where they'd see it if it tried to scale the cliff. If they couldn't see it...he didn't want to think about it.

"How much farther, Phelan?" Eron asked after turning back around. He felt dizzy and feared falling off the ledge.

"I'm not sure. All I see above us are clouds. I did spot a wider landing not too far away. Maybe we can stop there and plan the rest of the way."

"Sounds good," Eron said. Phelan led them slowly upwards. The ledge was not a straight shot up, but wound back and forth across the red rock.

After a little more than an hour, they found the landing that had been cut out from the wall. It was wide enough for them to lean back against the rock and not have their feet dangle over the edge. They ate some of their berries and edible leaves and rested.

The immense valley spread out before them, red, orange, and purple cascading across it.

"Beautiful, isn't it?" Phelan said. Eron nodded. Observed from this vantage point, it had a certain mismatched uniformity to it. Colors were spread out and clashed, but then were woven together to create a large cohesive tapestry. Eron turned away after a few moments.

"What's wrong?" Phelan said.

"Dizzy, that's all" Eron said. "I guess the change in altitude is affecting me. It didn't on the way down, but it's doing something to me now. It'll pass, I hope."

Eron closed his eyes and concentrated on Mina. He envisioned her gorgeous face in front of him. Holding her curls in his hands, he smelled her perfume. Her eyes were so full of life and love. Caressing her soft cheek, she smiled. His heart exploded with emotion.

Then he heard the screams. They were soft at first and he was too engrossed in Mina's beauty to pay much attention. But they were persistent and grew louder and louder until he couldn't ignore them. They sounded painful, and something like gunshots accompanied the screams.

Eron opened himself to the sounds and lost the vision of Mina in front of him. Suddenly he saw the Selection, though not his Selection. Ignoring his mother's direction and the armed soldiers, he crept to a place where he watched what was going on. The security force had cleared the area but somehow, he'd managed to avoid detection.

In front of him, several boys stood at one of the many paths leading into the forest, much like he'd done a few weeks ago. Ahead to his right was his brother. Timo looked nervous. He fidgeted back and forth, looking from side to side. Eron had never seen him so afraid of anything in his life. His big brother was always strong. He had to be, with their father gone in the Defense Force. Seeing Timo's fear eroded away his image of the hero his brother was to him. If he could've helped him he would, but he knew the guards were instructed to shoot to kill.

He was taught that in school last year, second semester.

Eron's eyes shot open. "What?" he said out loud. Phelan looked at him.

"Huh?" Phelan said.

"I was taught that in school. I was taught in school!"

"I'm not sure what you're saying, Eron. Care to clue me in?"

"I was taught about the guards shooting to kill. While in school. I was taught that!"

"You should've been taught all that stuff in school. I

thought we talked about this already. Whatever they're doing in Rippon is nothing compared to how we prepare in Greater Manthus. Lucky for you I came along."

"I was taught in school, Phelan. That means something. I know I was. Maybe something did happen to my memory."

Phelan looked out over the valley. "That's been my guess. I can't imagine your colony not preparing you."

"Oh, and you didn't come along. If you recall, I was the one who found you. And saved you. I'm not completely inept."

"I'd never say that," Phelan said. Both boys laughed.

"Ready to get back at it? I'd like to make the summit by nightfall. That is, if it's not too far above those clouds. We've only got a few more hours of daylight," said Phelan.

They left the landing and proceeded upward. The path quickly turned much more difficult.

Thirty-Three

The ledge grew narrow again. There were places where rock was missing, which meant the boys had to jump from one narrow outcrop to another. Pebbles and large rocks were scattered across the ledge. Here there were no grooves in the rock to hold onto. The wall was completely smooth, as if worn down over time. Eron hugged the rock face as best he could, but still almost slipped off more than once.

They got about fifteen meters from the landing they'd left and Eron looked down. "That's all? I thought we were higher than this by now. This is going to take forever!"

Phelan grunted, but kept moving forward.

Behind them came a screeching sound. Carefully turning, they watched as five large creatures circled next to them.

"Vulbores," Phelan said. "We've got to hurry! Those talons will kill us!"

Eron watched the vulbores dance in the air. Their wings were covered in dark purple skin. Dark ridges indicated the bones where the membranes attached. Eron had seen vulbores before, though they were the smaller blue ones, which were less deadly.

Like Phelan, he was concerned about the talons. Even the smaller ones excreted a deadly toxin from the tips of their talons that neutralized their prey. These larger ones probably held enough toxin to render the boys catatonic. And clinging to a narrow rock ledge several hundred meters above the valley was a bad place for that.

Eron looked back to the ledge and followed Phelan's lead. The other boy was moving quicker than before, and more recklessly.

"Phelan, slow down. If we fall because we miss a step, it would be just as bad as getting attacked by the vulbores."

"I'm willing to take the chance. I don't want those things near me!"

They crossed a narrow gap when Phelan's foot slipped, setting him off balance.

"Phelan!" Eron said.

"I'm all right. Just slipped." Screeching in the air behind him, one of the vulbores dove.

"Look out! Vulbore!" Eron said. Phelan turned just in time to swat at the vulbore with his arm. The thing shrieked and peeled off, turning back for another pass.

"Did you get scratched?" Eron asked.

Phelan shook his head. "No, I don't think so."

"Here it comes again!" Eron said.

Phelan saw it and swatted at it again, this time swinging forward from the ledge. He caught the vulbore on its bright purple beak, knocking its head violently to the side. Instead of flying away, it slammed into the cliff next to Phelan. He swung his arms, trying to regain his balance.

"Phelan!" Eron said. He was too far away to grab him, but he continued to shuffle across the ledge toward him. Phelan whirled his arms, teetering on the ledge before his body slammed back against the cliff. His chest heaved in and out as he clung to the wall.

"I'm ok!" he said. Next to him, the vulbore thrashed then slid off the ledge, falling helplessly down. They were too high up to hear the thud when it crashed through the trees to the ground below.

The remaining vulbores screeched madly at the sight of their fallen comrade. They circled in the air, dipping in and out of each other's paths.

"We've got to do something!" Eron said. "They're gonna attack!"

Phelan caught his breath. "We have to go back down. We can't fight them off up here. We're not that far from the landing. If we go back, we can at least get better footing."

Eron started for the landing, careful not to misstep. The vulbores screeched in the air behind him, threatening the boys. Eron kept moving as the vulbores broke from their circle and dove at them. They seemed wary of getting too close as they veered away before they reached the boys. Still their cries and the sight of those large talons coming after them were frightening. Eron almost slid off the ledge, but caught his foot on a small rock, stabilizing himself. He thought about swinging his staff at the vulbores, but decided taking it off his back would be too difficult.

Despite the screaming vulbores swooping, the boys finally made it to the landing. Eron grabbed his staff and pushed back at the vulbores. They gained confidence and flew closer to the boys, one almost catching Eron's arm in its talons. At the last second, he turned one aside with his staff and it collided with the wall next to him.

Phelan held out his knife, hoping for a chance to stab or slice at one of them, though that meant getting dangerously close.

"We have to hold them off, Eron! Maybe kill another one or two to scare them off. We can't move without getting rid of them!"

Eron waited for a vulbore that broke from the circle and dove fast at him, its long beak open in an awful screech with its talons out, ready to strike. When it was within reach, he swung the staff, thumping it on the head. It crashed on the landing in front of him. Phelan pounced, stabbing it in the head with his knife. The blade slid through its weak skull, piercing the brain. Its body convulsed as it died. Phelan kicked it off the landing to the valley below.

The three remaining vulbores were whipped into a frenzy. They screeched louder and broke from their circle to attack the boys. Eron swung his staff back and forth, trying to scare them from getting any closer, and almost struck Phelan, who had to duck twice to avoid the staff.

As one unit, the large purple vulbores turned back and dove at them again, talons and wings blurring together. Eron swung his staff, striking flesh and bone. Feeling resistance, he swung again and again, hoping Phelan was not in the way. He heard the other boy scream. Fear ran through him. *They got Phelan!* he thought. His anger fueled his swings and he struck at the vulbores again, staff connecting with a thud against solid bodies.

Before long, two of the three vulbores lay flopping on the ground in front of them. The third one flew away screeching, its flight hampered as it lurched through the sky.

Phelan stabbed one of the vulbores in the back. It flapped its wings, knocking the other one off the ledge. He stabbed several times, spilling bright pink blood. With one last thrust of his blade, he pulled out the knife and pushed the vulbore off the landing.

"Are you hurt? Did they get you?" Eron said. He dropped his staff on the ground.

"Yeah, I'm hurt, but it wasn't because of them!" Phelan said. "You hit me with that stupid staff! Watch what you're doing with that thing!"

"I was trying to push them back! I couldn't see what was going on. You can't blame me for that," said Eron.

"Look, whatever. It's done with. They're gone."

Both boys fell to the ground, breathing heavy, leaning against the wall. Little food and water and the climb up the cliff had taken its toll on them.

"I hope we don't come across more of those," Eron said. "I don't have the energy left."

Phelan rubbed his eyes. "I agree."

Thirty-Four

The boys didn't rest long.

"We've got to get moving, Eron. We can't wait here like this."

Eron ached all over. His arms, his legs, his entire body was stiff with pain. It hurt to open his eyes.

"I know. I'm sore. How much farther do you think it is? I'm exhausted."

"I think we've still got a couple hours' worth of a climb to go."

Eron rolled his eyes.

"I know. I'm not looking forward to it, either. We need to go up or down, but we can't stay here. Soon, others will be climbing this path and we don't want to be here when they do. I told you this was the most difficult part of the journey. We're too close to give up now."

Eron grunted, pushed himself up and steadied himself with the staff. Extending his hand, he helped Phelan up.

"Thanks," Phelan said. "Now if there are no more obstacles, we're good to go."

Phelan led as they climbed back up along the cliff's ledge. When they approached the place where they had encountered the vulbores, Eron looked up at the sky, half expecting to find more of them. Except for the yellow clouds, the sky was clear. He thought he saw a flicker of light and his heart jumped. The last thing they needed was rain. He waited for the thunder, but no sound came.

"Did you see that, Phelan?" he said. They were making good time, considering the treacherous ledge they were climbing. Both boys tried to ignore the possibility of falling.

"See what? Are there more vulbores?"

"No. I thought I saw lightning."

Phelan stopped and looked at the yellow clouds swirling above. "I don't see anything. Hopefully it was something else; we have no escape from the rain. That's the last thing we need."

"Agreed," Eron said.

They went back to climbing. It was perilous in places and they feared they'd need to turn around. By chance and a few daring leaps, they managed to stay alive. As they approached the bottom of the yellow clouds, they saw it.

"There!" Eron said pointing at the flash in the clouds. "Lightning!" As soon as he said it, thunder boomed loud, vibrating the cliff. The deep, deafening boom reverberated in their ears.

"We have to hurry!" Phelan said. Eron barely heard him. Phelan pointed up and hurried along the ledge. He abruptly turned and almost slipped off. Rocks tumbled down as he tried to regain his footing.

Again, thunder boomed around them, shaking the cliff. Eron held his hands over his ears. The motion threatened to send him off balance. He leaned forward and fell face first against the wall. It hurt, but he was alive.

They made their way up through the clouds, the air growing colder the instant they reached them. Soon they felt the burning sensation travel slowly from head to toe.

"Eron, do you feel that?"

"Yeah, is it the cloud?"

Lightning streaked through the clouds followed by booming thunder. Eron's teeth rattled.

"I think so. We need to hurry!"

"Are we near the top?" Eron said.

"I have no idea. It doesn't matter. Hurry, Eron! We're in trouble!"

Eron's skin burned like a horrible sunburn. He watched as the pale skin on his arms turned pink. His eyes stung, making it difficult to see.

They pushed on out of necessity, reckless.

"My eyes!" Phelan screamed. "They're burning! Come on, Eron, hurry!"

Eron fumbled through the cloud. His skin burned hotter. His eyes were nearly blinded, exposed to the toxic moisture that blurred his vision.

Phelan gained some distance from Eron and was a bit higher. Eron lost him through the cloud and stinging vision, but then from above he heard Phelan's screams.

No! Eron thought. *Not Phelan! Not him!*

Eron felt his way through the cloud, finding a foothold wherever he could. He had to get to Phelan. The other boy screamed again and again, but sounded different.

The air around Eron changed, growing a bit warmer. His eyes stung, but not as bad as before. He opened them wider and his sight returned. The yellow tinge of the cloud was gone. He continued climbing towards Phelan.

Reaching his hand up for the cliff face, there wasn't anything for Eron to hold onto and he fell forward into the tall grass. He had reached the top.

Phelan ran around the summit, screaming and leaping up and down.

"We made it, Eron! We made it! My skin's starting to cool down! We made it!" Phelan ran to him and lifted him off the ground. Eron's skin still burned, but the intensity lessened. His eyes didn't hurt as bad when he opened them.

"We made it!" Eron said in a weak voice. "We made it!"

They jumped around in the tall grass, looking down on the clouds below them. Lightning flashed in the clouds and muffled thunder boomed.

Thirty-Five

By the time their eyes no longer burned, night had settled over them. Stars shone in the darkening sky. The pink moon was coming up bright and full. Tall red grass waved in the cool wind. In the distance, the forest started again. They decided to wait until the morning, but it called to them like a beacon.

"There it is, Eron. Our last challenge. We make it through the forest, and the end will be ours. I hear there's a fair waiting. If we aren't there within thirty days' time, they pack up and leave. Soldiers are stationed there and like when we started, if any boy tries to get out after the time is up, they're shot or driven back here. Those are the Forgotten; some of them, anyway. The rest just never made it to the end and are stuck here."

Eron looked past the field at the treetops. They looked black, not vibrant like the trees he was used to. He really couldn't tell for sure, though, since they were so far away and it was dark.

"Where do you think Bello is?" Eron said.

"I don't know. He might be behind us in the valley. I hope so. We'll be out of here well before he ever finds us again, if that's the case. If not, then he's in there somewhere," said Phelan, pointing to the forest ahead of them. "And if he's in there, we'll need to be extra careful. I suspect he'll try something."

"But how do we know where he is? I'm pretty sure he'll come after me. And you, too, I guess. What a pain he's become," Eron said.

Phelan nodded. "Yes, he has. You need to take care of him if or when he shows up again. Be strong. Sometimes, some of us aren't meant to live through it.

"I think of it as forced evolution. The strongest males survive while the weaker ones get tossed aside. We have too many males on this planet. We have to keep balance. They say that's what happened on Earth; it became so out of balance that it couldn't sustain the wild shifts much longer. Moderation, Eron; that's how things proceed and endure. Balance in nature and life produces the best results. That's why we're here. Forced balance to create a balanced planet. It's worked for a couple hundred years so far."

Eron thought about Phelan's words. Being so close to the end had turned the other boy into a philosopher. Or maybe he was opening up, feeling the stress of the Selection fading since they were almost finished.

"But why are the numbers so out of balance? Is it a natural thing? If it was started like this on Earth, who are we to upset the natural order? Shouldn't we accept the situation?"

"Hmm, good question. I never knew you to have such deep thoughts!" Phelan laughed. Eron smiled.

"Yeah, well, normally I don't. You made me think, that's all. Even now, I'm still so confused about the Selection. I've been given no answers, yet forced into this terrible process all the same."

"You keep saying that," Phelan said. He sat in the

grass holding his knees up to his chest. The pink moon glow illuminated his blue face. "I think you know more than you're aware of. I've thought about this for a while now. My guess is it was the trauma of your brother's time in the Selection. Since you don't know for sure whether he's alive or dead, it broke your mind. As a safety mechanism, your mind either erased the memories, or made them inaccessible, which is almost as bad as being erased."

"I wish I knew for sure. I think you might be kinda right. Timo was my brother. Is my brother. And all the years of schooling? Those would be hard to forget."

"Maybe it's some kind of selective amnesia brought on by extreme stress or trauma. Such as your brother being shot."

"So, you're a doctor now? They must be so proud of you in Greater Manthus," Eron said. He turned away from Phelan and looked up at the sky. Silence hung thick between them.

"I'm sorry if I offended you, Eron, it was just a thought. I don't know why you can't remember those things, but, I'm sure you were taught them. You had to have known about the Selection."

"I wish I could remember," Eron said.

Phelan nodded. He ran his fingers through the grass before speaking.

"Ever think you're gonna die out here?" he asked.

"What the...no! I mean I guess it could happen but I'm not planning on it."

"I know I'm not going to die. I'm determined. I'm resourceful."

"And you've got me!"

Phelan laughed. "Yeah...and I've got you."

In the still night air, the sound of craates howling carried across the plain. A faint scream emerged from the forest. Both boys turned toward the sound.

"We're not out of this yet," Eron said. "We still have to cross through that."

Thirty-Six

When the sun rose bright red and warm, the boys set off. The sky was bright and cloudless. No animals chittered; the wind blowing across the tall red grass was the only sound. It rippled back and forth like waves on an ocean.

Eron's stomach grumbled.

"Phelan, we need to find some food soon. And water."

"I agree," he said, waving towards the plain. "I'm sure we'll find something in there."

As they walked in silence listening to the wind, Eron looked up as a black figure raced across the plain to their right.

"Phelan, over there! It's another Forgotten!" Eron said. He pointed his staff.

"I didn't see it. It's not like there's many places to hide up here. Which way was it going?"

"From there," Eron pointed, "to there. It looked just like the one we've seen before."

"The same Forgotten?" Phelan said.

"That's my guess; at least, I hope so. Then we'd know what we're dealing with. If it's a different one..." Eron trailed off when the Forgotten reappeared. However, this time, it stood erect and seemed to be looking at the boys.

"Phelan," Eron said.

"I see it, Eron. I think you're right. It looks like the one."

It raised its arms in a V, then pointed towards the forest before disappearing in the tall grass. The boys stood mesmerized, waiting for it to emerge again. After several minutes, they continued on when it didn't appear.

"What's it want?" Eron said.

"How would I know? I've got no idea why it's paying attention to us. We need to keep our distance and make sure to watch for it. I'd hate to be ambushed."

They continued towards the forest, every few meters, Eron scanning the landscape.

By late afternoon, the boys closed in on the forest. They saw individual trees and the underbrush.

"Almost there," Eron said. "I can't wait. I need food and shade. The sun is pretty bright up here." His cracked lips bled a little. They were burned and chapped from the ever-present brutal wind. It hurt to talk. What he wouldn't give for shelter from the wind.

"I told you, coward, I was going to kill you."

The boys jumped. Eron's heart raced.

Bello stood behind them.

"Where did you come from?" Eron said. He held his staff across his body.

"Does it matter? You and blue face made it all the way up here, only to die. By me!" Bello said. He charged the boys, knocking Phelan to the ground and winding him.

Eron swung his staff and missed, giving Bello the chance to knock him in the jaw.

"I'm finally going to kill you! I've waited long

enough. Blue face's death will be on your hands. You should never have brought him into this!"

"Into what?" Eron said. Rubbing his jaw, he backed away from Bello.

"Into our fight, coward! Only the weak need someone else to help them. The strong only need themselves."

Phelan tried to scramble away and Bello kicked him. When he saw the knife at Phelan's belt, he dropped to his knees, punched Phelan, and took it. "You won't need this, blue face," Bello said and tossed it far away in the grass. "My hands are all I need." Phelan struggled to get up. Bello punched him in the face, sending blood trickling from his nose. Phelan held both hands to his nose, writhing on the ground.

Eron jumped up. "Get off him! This is our fight!" he said to Bello. Phelan squirmed, but the larger boy pinned him to the ground with one hand. He turned to grin at Eron, then punched Phelan several times in the face. The flesh around his eyes grew dark and puffy. Bello let the boy go and stood, towering over Eron. Phelan curled into the fetal position, covering his face.

"What are you gonna do, coward? Finally found some courage? I doubt it." He dropped his hands to his sides and took a few steps toward Eron.

"Don't make me do something I don't want to, Bello! I've not hurt you yet because it's not right. And it won't happen here unless you make me." Eron's lips stung. As he spoke, they bled trails of crimson down his chin.

"Unless I make you? Spoken like a true coward. If you had any strength in you, you'd strike first when you have the advantage. But you're a coward. And cowards don't do that, do they? That's why you don't deserve to make it to the end. That's why I get to kill you."

He lunged at Eron. The smaller boy countered with his staff, though there wasn't much room between them to strike with much force and the blow glanced off Bello, ineffective.

Bello slammed into Eron. Yelling, Bello chided him. "Is that all? I expected you to be better at this by now. It's time to die!" He pushed Eron to the ground and pinned him, kneeing Eron in the legs and groin. Eron struggled to free himself, but the larger boy held his arms to the ground.

"Get off me!" Eron said.

"Not today. I finally get to kill you. Cowards don't make it through the Selection. I'll make sure you don't." Bello smashed his head into Eron's nose. After a dull crunch, blood flowed from his nose and streamed down his cheeks. The blood seemed to excite Bello.

"That's it, coward, bleed for me! Only cowards bleed like that!" He slammed his head into Eron's nose again. Eron screamed. He fought to free himself, but the more he struggled, the harder Bello clamped on his wrists.

Blood covered Eron's eyes and face. He could see it on Bello's head. The larger boy looked down on him with crazed eyes. Eron gathered enough courage to speak.

"Bello, you don't have to do this. We can survive together. You don't have to kill me."

"Shut up, coward! You will die! I owe you for what

you've done to me! You won't get away again."

Bello let go of Eron's wrists and pulled the boy up to his feet. "I'm gonna teach you a lesson. A real man dies facing his foe. He dies on his feet fighting back. Fight me, coward! Fight!" Eron staggered, unable to make sense of what was going on. Blood obscured his vision. Excruciating pain radiated outward from his nose. His sight faded in and out.

"Coward! Fight back like a real man! Come on!" Bello screamed. The larger boy stood a few steps back from Eron with his hands down at his side, waiting for Eron to make his move. He couldn't. Pain overwhelmed him.

"Bello, we don't have to do this. We can live alongside each—" Bello cut him off, punching him in the stomach, forcing him to double over.

"Quit talking, coward! Your whole family is nothing but cowards. Your dad abandoned you, and your brother screamed like a coward. He never was man enough for the Selection. I don't know why you thought you were. Cowards don't get to live."

Eron shook as Bello screamed at him. He thought of Timo. He thought of all he wanted in life. Anger rose and pushed the pain away.

"I'm done with you calling me a coward, Bello. I won't stand by any longer—" Eron began.

Phelan was disregarded by both Bello and Eron and he slunk through the grass, searching for his knife. Eron's words were cut short as Phelan's blade plunged into Bello's temple and he fell over, eyes rolling back into his skull.

Dead.

Thirty-Seven

Eron opened his eyes to the sight of bright red and orange leaves above him. A gracer flew across his view. His face was engulfed in throbbing pain; pressure in his head to the breaking point. His legs burned, alerting him of more injuries he was unaware of.

"About time you got up. We're starting to get behind schedule. I'm not going to become a Forgotten."

The voice sounded familiar.

"Connor?" Eron said.

A blue face peered at him. "Nope. It's just me." He squinted at Phelan through his puffy eyes.

"Phelan, where am I?" Panic set in. "Where's Bello? Watch out for Bello!" Eron said.

"You're in bad shape, Eron. Don't you remember what happened?"

Eron tried to shake his head, but visions held his attention.

Soldiers. Shots. Timo.

His brother had turned, intending to run home. Nearby soldiers threatened to open fire if he didn't go into the forest. Timo froze. He looked to either side. One of the soldiers had an itchy trigger finger and let loose a couple rounds. Timo slumped over, screaming in agony. Eron was frightened by the deafening screams. His strong older brother was in pain and he couldn't help. To his left, he heard laughter. Turning from his brother's screams, he saw a faint glimpse of someone else in hiding. Someone else was there to watch the boys off.

It was Bello.

"Bello," Eron said in a hoarse voice.

"Yeah. Bello attacked us. He ambushed us. You tried talking to him, and he beat you up pretty good. Got me, too. Last time he does that. I got him for you, Eron. I did what you couldn't. I killed Bello."

Eron closed his eyes. "No! Why? Why did you kill him? He should've been allowed to live!" Even as he said it, he knew it was a lie. Bello was there when they shot his brother—and laughed. Bello was after Eron, too, and wouldn't stop until he killed him. Bello was the one that needed to die. But why? Why did anyone have to die? The Selection was wrong. Nature should go its own way. Tampering with it led to serious consequences.

"He had to die, Eron. You're too soft sometimes. You killed others to survive; how was he different? Why should he have lived?"

Eron's mind reeled. He had no answers. Killing wasn't the solution. Weeding out males was wrong. Why didn't anyone see that?

"We all deserve to live," Eron said. It was difficult to talk through the pain. Dried blood cracked on his face. "We should all have the chance to live. All of us." He coughed hard, his body trying to expel whatever was inside. "Even Laird. And Bello."

"You're wrong, Eron. We do what we can to survive. Even if it's not something you always agree with. Survival isn't easy. Sometimes we have to make extremely difficult decisions. Sometimes we do things we don't like just to get by. Bello needed to die."

Phelan walked away. Eron waited for him to return and when he did, Phelan held his cupped hands out to him.

"Here, drink. I found some water. You need to get your energy back quick. I've seen the Forgotten roaming around in the forest. I'm going to need your help if he comes for us. And we're so close to the end. Two days, three tops. Then we're free. No more killing, no more worrying if someone is after us."

"And Mina," Eron said.

"Yeah, and Mina. Come on; drink, Eron. We've got to get moving."

Eron struggled to stand, almost falling over. His head throbbed. Most likely, his nose was broken, and if not set soon, it would be crooked for the rest of his life. Getting to the end was more crucial now than ever. What if Mina was disgusted by his appearance? He couldn't risk it.

"Where are we?" he said to Phelan. The other boy was clearing the way for them.

"In the forest, of course. Not too far in. After Bello attacked us and I killed him, I brought you here. The Forgotten has been more active, too. He's a bit bolder. Keeps showing up and pointing the way for us. I'm not sure if he's trying to help or telling us to go."

Eron turned to look through the forest, hoping to see the Forgotten. Electric pain caused him to stumble. Phelan ran to him, lifting him up under his arms.

"Hey, it's all right; I've got you," he said to Eron. Though Eron was smaller, Phelan struggled to hold him up.

"I'm sorry, Phelan. I should've done it. I couldn't kill him, and it cost us. We're both injured, and getting to the end will be much harder now. I'm so sorry."

Phelan shook his head. "Don't apologize. It's who you are. You aren't made for this kind of thing. Lucky for you we met. We make a good team."

"We sure do," Eron said. If only his family could see him now. They'd know he'd become a man. He was going to make it. He found a new friend, and together they battled beasts and boys to make their way to the end. When he finally was reunited with Mina, if she looked past his facial deformity, they'd live a long and happy life together.

"Eron, how strong do you think you are? Can you make it the rest of the way?" Phelan asked.

"I have to. I won't lie, Phelan; I'm in a lot of pain, but I have to make it."

"Keep that thought, Eron. Use it to push yourself. If your mind decides you've given up, the rest of your body will follow. We're close now. Soon, Eron. Soon."

"I can't wait, Phelan. I hope we're done with problems. I'm not sure how much more I can take."

Thirty-Eight

The Forgotten stalked them. Eron saw him to his left. He stood watching them from a distance. Once, he stared directly at Phelan and growled. The fierce and deep growl made the boys hesitate, expecting an attack, but he remained still. He seemed to prefer to keep his distance from them. They'd be all right if they didn't have to fight another enemy.

Later in the day, the Forgotten stood a little closer than earlier and stopped. He stared at Eron, his head tilted. He was silent. Then he opened his eyes wide and became agitated. He jumped up and down, beating his chest. Waving his arms, he looked like an animal caught in a trap. Eron's grip on his staff tightened, the muscles in his arms becoming tense.

"Phelan, what's he doing?" he said.

"I don't know. Did you do something to him?"

"No! I didn't tease him. I've been watching for him, but nothing else. Did you do something to tick him off?"

"No, but I might if he doesn't leave us alone." Phelan had removed his knife and was tossing it in the air, making a great show to the Forgotten. He continued to growl and jump around, but didn't seem frightened. Eron thought for sure he heard a scream come from him which sounded very much like Timo, but he knew that was impossible. He closed his eyes and covered them with his hand, trying to clear his mind of Timo.

"Phelan, do you know where we're going? We've been walking all day and I don't think we've gotten far at all."

"We haven't. With you in such bad shape we haven't made much progress. I could leave you and make it to the end just fine." Phelan stopped and grinned at Eron. "We're through the hardest part. Why do I need you?"

"What?" Eron said. "You're gonna leave me? After all we've been through? I thought you were better than that."

Phelan's smile widened. "I'm just telling you what I could do."

Eron shook his head. Sometimes Phelan confused him. The entire Selection confused him.

"Hey, over there," said Phelan pointing to the side, "I think it's a craate. I hate those things."

Eron watched as a craate stalked in the brush, turning toward them, long fangs bared as a warning.

"There's bound to be more," Eron said. "They always travel in packs."

"I've never understood that. Why travel in packs where the weakest one could expose the entire group to danger? Why not travel alone where it can fight and live or die based on its own merits? Weak animals leach off the stronger ones."

Eron narrowed his eyes. "What are you trying to say? Am I the weak one that's exposing you to danger? Why don't you come out and say it? Why not leave me?"

"Eron, what are you saying? I'm talking about

craates, not us! Calm down."

Phelan's words didn't sound genuine. There was something in his tone that didn't sit well with Eron. Something changed with Phelan. Maybe it was all in Eron's head. He'd been through a lot. He was past his breaking point. The boy he was at the start of the Selection seemed so naive and unprepared compared to the man he was now. He'd moved past being afraid all the time.

The craate howled. Four more craates had joined the first one, the pack facing them.

"Oh no," Eron said. "The pack. Get ready, Phelan."

The other boy laughed. "You know what? I am ready."

His voice was strange. Eron turned just in time to see the other boy lunging at him with his knife. Eron ducked the slash, stepping to the side.

"Phelan! What are you doing?"

Picking himself off the ground, the blue boy dusted himself off. "I have told you, Eron, to survive the Selection, you have to do whatever you can. I intend on making it out of here. Your usefulness is over. You're keeping me back. I will not be one of the Forgotten," he said, waving his knife. "I won't, Eron. Sometimes tough choices need to be made. You've been incapable of making any since we met. I figured this would happen at some point, and now is the time."

Eron's eyes were large, white circles of fear.

"But, Phelan! We're friends! We've helped each other survive! We've killed others to protect each other. How can you do this?" Eron's arms shook. His heart raced. With craates behind him, a Forgotten stalking them, and Phelan threatening him, he lost hope of ever seeing Mina again.

"Phelan, please. Don't do this. We can work it out. I'll leave you; go my own way if I have to. Just please, don't do this," Eron said.

Phelan tossed his knife back and forth in front of him. His dark blue lips were curled in an evil grin. "Eron, you're too weak for this world. I thought maybe you'd grow out of it, but I don't think so. You aren't made to survive the Selection. That's clear to me now. Maybe Bello was right about you after all."

"No! He was wrong, and so are you! I'm not weak! I'm not a coward!"

Phelan walked slowly around Eron as if circling his prey. "Yes, you are Eron. You've known this all along, haven't you? Saving me when we met felt like a fluke. Since then, you've demonstrated how weak you are. Your unwillingness to kill when it's necessary is a big sign to me how much you don't belong."

Craates closed in behind them. Leaves crunched and twigs snapped as the pack approached the boys. Phelan turned when one of the craates growled. It was a couple of meters away and the pack spread out, blocking their escape.

"Because of you, Eron, we're in this mess! Your weakness will kill us both if I don't kill you first."

Eron spun, his staff warding off the craates. They dodged but kept their formation.

"That's not true, Phelan! Neither one of us has to die. If we work together like we've done before, we can survive this and anything else that comes our way. Together we're better. Alone, we die."

"Then that's the risk I'm willing to take," said Phelan. He lunged at Eron just as the craates rushed them.

Thirty-Nine

In an instant, Eron's world changed. His partner throughout the Selection had turned on him. Already beat down from his fight with Bello, Eron didn't have much stamina left.

And then there were the craates.

As Eron dodged Phelan's lumbering attack, he could hear the snarling craates moving closer. There was no turning his back on them. He had Phelan with his knife, waiting to plunge it into his weakened body and the pack of craates threatening him. For the first time during his journey through the Selection, Eron felt certain death was near.

"I'm going to do to you what Bello never could! Did you honestly think I was going to let you live, Eron? This is survival! It's you or me, but not both of us. Weaklings are meant to die here. And that is what you are."

"Phelan, listen to yourself! We've helped each other. You needed me to save you from the craates. You couldn't have done it on your own. We've needed each other since we met. Don't you see that?" Eron's head pounded. Soon the craates would be on them, and he'd have to decide how far he was willing to go in order to survive. If he could.

"Shut up!" Phelan said, punching Eron in the mouth. A shock of pain pulsated through Eron's face.

Bright flashes of light erupted in front of him. He fell backwards, landing on the ground, gasping for breath and thrashing.

"No, Phelan, please! This isn't you," he said through short, painful breaths.

"What do you know? How can you possibly know me?" Phelan stood over Eron, knife pointed at his chest. "You know nothing about me! I was taught to survive. Not to make friends. You're only useful to me as the means to an end. Now that end has come, and I don't need you anymore. I've known since we met I'd probably kill you. If you were a true survivor worthy of living, you would've left me in that tree. But you didn't."

Eyes shut tight, remembering the day they met, Eron saw how scared Phelan looked in the tree, waiting for help to arrive. This couldn't be the same person.

Around them, the craates crept closer. Growls grew louder and snarls more menacing. Eron saw movement at the edge of his vision, though with Phelan over him, he was reluctant to tear his gaze from his former friend.

"I saved you because that's what we do. We save each other. We humans have to believe that lives matter. All life matters. If we take that lightly, we lose what makes us human. We become nothing more than animals."

"Look at me!" Phelan screamed. "Do I look human to you?"

A create lunged, snarling and nearly ripping off a piece of Eron's ear. Phelan laughed. "I should let them take you out."

Eron screamed. He wanted so badly to be free of this moment. Overwhelming tragedy had already affected his mind and this pushed the limits of his sanity.

"Yes, you do look human Phelan. You're as human as me or anyone else."

"Then you're as dumb as Bello believed you were. We kill to live, Eron. That's all it's ever been. Only the strongest among us earn the right, and you aren't one of us. You're the kind we feed on."

The craates moved even closer, snarling. Phelan looked at the beasts, then back at Eron. He flicked his knife in their direction, forcing them back.

"And we're right where we started. Tell me, how do you save me now? How do you free me from them?"

Eron said nothing.

"I thought so," Phelan said.

In a slow, deliberate movement, Phelan picked Eron's staff from the ground and swung it in a wide arc, striking several craates. They yelped and shrieked, backing away.

"That's it, you stupid things! Get back! Get away!" He swung the staff again in a large circle, pushing the craates back. He caught one with the staff and fractured its jaw. The craate howled and thrashed before Phelan crushed its skull with the staff, ending its life.

"You see, Eron! Only the strong survive! I'm the stronger one, not them. Not you!"

A craate rushed Phelan and nipped him in the leg. The boy screamed and swung the staff, missing the craate entirely.

"I'll kill you for that!" he yelled. The craate growled, its long fangs dripping with saliva.

Eron raised himself slowly to sit.

"Don't you dare move, Eron! I'm not done with you." Phelan spat the words at him.

Two craates charged Phelan. They barked and snarled when they lunged at him. The boy swung the staff to fend off the attack, but instead of hitting them, he smacked Eron in the ribs. Eron doubled over from the blow. Phelan lost his grip on the staff and it landed next to Eron.

Phelan stumbled backwards a few steps before catching his balance.

"Don't you dare pick that up!" He threw his knife at Eron. Its long, bloodied blade sunk into Eron's left hand, pinning him to the ground.

Eron screamed. Phelan jumped towards him and pulled the knife free. "That's not for you!" he said. He then picked up the staff and pushed back on the craates until they were a few meters away.

Phelan turned to Eron. "Now it's time to die."

Forty

Phelan approached Eron with the knife pointed towards him. He left the staff on the ground near the wounded craates.

"I've had enough of you, Eron. It's your time to die. Like I said, only the strong get to live."

"Phelan, please. No, don't do this." He held up his hands to ward off the impending attack.

Eron saw a flash of black race through the forest around them. A craate yelped. Then another. And another until their snarls went silent.

Phelan turned, looking for the source of the craates' pain. He saw the flash of black. "Stupid Forgotten!"

Eron took a chance and lunged at Phelan's legs, knocking the boy down. He climbed on top of him, trying to hold his arms down, but Phelan was much stronger and resisted.

"Now you decide to show some courage," Phelan said. "Too bad it's too late for you." He pushed Eron's hands away and tossed him aside with ease.

"No more games, Eron!" Phelan tackled him to the ground and punched him in the face, his nose becoming bloodier and more painful than he thought possible. Eron tried to block the blows as Phelan kept pummeling him.

"Die, Eron! You're too weak for this world!" Phelan screamed. Spit flew out of his mouth.

He screamed, and in the back of his mind he thought of Timo. He could hear Timo's screams and he understood his brother's fear. He understood his pain. He'd soon understand his death.

"Goodbye, Eron," said Phelan as he raised his fist in the air while clutching the boy's throat.

Eron's vision was obscured by a large black shape that flew in from his right side and tossed Phelan off him. The creature snarled. At first, Eron thought it was one of the craates, but it was too bulky.

He pushed himself off the ground, expecting any moment to be taken by the craates. When he turned his groggy and painful head towards the black figure, he saw it was one of the Forgotten.

"Get off me!" Phelan screamed. The beast snarled and roared loud, his head rearing back. Then, with giant black fists, he struck Phelan in the face and body. The boy didn't stand a chance against the much larger and more ferocious Forgotten.

"Stop! Leave me alone! Eron! Eron, please help me!" Phelan said. For a moment, Eron thought about attacking the Forgotten, but his fuzzy mind slowed his actions.

"Help?" Eron said in a weak voice. Blood dripped down his lips to his chin.

The Forgotten pummeled Phelan despite the boy's protests. Thick black arms raised and lowered, smacking into the boy with a sick rhythm. Deep thuds sounded with each blow. Bones cracked. Blood sprayed.

Eron watched it unfold in front of him, his mind not registering exactly what was going on. It was like the time he stole some of his mother's alcohol and drank much more than he should've and everything was blurry and spinning. Like then, he lost focus on what was going on. He knew Phelan was under the Forgotten, but his ability to care or act vanished.

Phelan screamed as the Forgotten attacked him. He tore into the boy.

"Eron, please help me! I'm sorry. We can finish this. We can make it to the end!" Phelan screamed. The Forgotten smacked him in the mouth, sending a tooth flying. He continued to pummel Phelan.

Something in Eron snapped. He lunged at the Forgotten, barely knocking him off Phelan. He couldn't let him kill his friend. Betrayal or not, he vowed to save lives, not end them. He kicked at the Forgotten. He howled and ran a few meters away until he stopped and turned around, waiting. He was covered in Phelan's blood, matting his thick hair with gore.

The Forgotten cocked his head at Eron, the boy felt as though he saw recognition in his face. The Forgotten's eyes widened, then he stepped towards Eron. What Bello had started and Phelan continued, he was sure the creature was going to finish.

"Kill me and be done with it. I can't go on anymore," Eron said. The creature raised his fists as if to strike him. Eron lowered his head.

"Timo, I come to find you now," Eron said.

The creature halted. He relaxed and dropped his arms.

"Go!" he screamed at Eron. "Go that way and never turn back." The voice was familiar. Timo's? But that wasn't possible. Eron's stressed brain teetered on the edge of insanity.

"I said go!" the Forgotten said when Eron didn't move. When he stood and looked at the creature, he appeared to be crying. "Go that way! Don't turn back. Ever! This is not for you. You get to live."

Eron was frozen by his words.

The creature roared. "I said leave!" He lunged at Eron, backing him up, and Eron tripped over Phelan. He landed on his back, and Phelan leapt on him.

Bloody from the Forgotten's beating, Phelan struck at Eron, who covered his face and blindly punched and kicked. The Forgotten roared. Eron struck Phelan in the ribs and the boy buckled. He pushed Phelan upwards and knocked the boy off him.

"Please stop this! We can work it out. There's no need for us to kill each other." Eron held Phelan's arms to the ground. The blue boy hissed at him.

"Let me go, and I'll kill you Eron. You're weak and don't deserve to live." Eron held steady.

"It doesn't have to end this way, Phelan! This is wrong!"

Phelan struggled against the hold and pushed Eron off him. He struck the other boy several times in the face.

"I told you I'm going to kill you, Eron." Phelan lunged with his knife. It missed its mark and Eron grabbed his wrist, intending on forcing it from his hand. Instead in the struggle, he pushed the blade into Phelan's stomach. The blue boy's eyes grew wide.

"No, Phelan! No I didn't mean it! We can both live through this!" Phelan fell to the ground.

Blood gurgled in Phelan's mouth. He turned his head. He mouthed the word, "Eron," before his eyes closed.

"Phelan, no! It was an accident. I'm so sorry!" He lay his head on the blue boy's chest, sobbing. "No, no, no, no," he said. He listened as the final breath left Phelan.

Eron closed his eyes, unable to move. If the Forgotten wanted to kill him, he'd not fight back. Phelan's betrayal cut deep. In his naivety, Eron trusted a stranger. This stranger saved him and helped him through so much and for what? To turn on him and try to kill him? It wasn't right. None of what he'd experienced was right.

Minutes later when he finally looked up, he saw the Forgotten. He expected him to attack. Instead, he pointed towards the end of Eron's nightmare. Soon, if his will held out, he'd be at Victory Point. He looked down at Phelan's body and cried out.

Behind him, the Forgotten roared and howled.

Forty-One

Eron stumbled through the forest, unsure of where he was or where he needed to go. Nothing seemed right. Unrelenting pain accompanied him with each step. Breathing hurt. Everything hurt.

Inside, he felt a deep dark pit beginning to grow. It threatened to overwhelm him if he wasn't careful. Guarding against this new threat would be almost impossible.

What he'd experienced was horrific. He didn't know how long ago it had happened. Sunlight still shone through the trees; it couldn't have been that long ago.

"Phelan, which way do we go?" he said out loud, then realized what he'd done. The pit widened. His head throbbed as though threatening to implode. Dried blood crusted his face and shirt. He tried to wipe it off, but without water it was a useless gesture.

He wondered how much more he could take. It seemed that he had nothing left, yet there was so far to go. The will to fight, the strength to endure was almost completely drained from him.

It was difficult to see anything with his eyes nearly swollen shut, but he thought there was an opening in the dense forest. When he approached the clearing, it turned out to be a stream cutting the land in half. He stumbled towards the stream and fell on his knees at the water's edge.

The swift red water flowed left to right. It looked wonderful as though it carried the secret to life itself. Dipping his hands in the cool water, he splashed it on his face. He rinsed much of the blood away. Then he bent over, almost falling in, and drank. The cool water soothed his parched throat. A cold sensation trailed down his throat into his aching stomach.

When he drank his fill, he rolled over on his back and gazed up at the trees above. The sun was low in the sky and darkness would be on him soon. He decided to stay where he was for the night, fearing what other dangers still lay in wait.

He tried to process what he'd been through.

What happened to Phelan? The betrayal was devastating. His friend turning on him was a torture he didn't see coming. Why did he try to kill him? Weren't they friends? Weren't they helping each other to survive the Selection so they'd live long lives, each with a new bride and children and everything else that came with it?

The look in Phelan's eyes was powerful. He meant what he said. Every word he screamed at Eron was hurtful and Phelan believed what he was saying. Did they teach that at Greater Manthus? Is that how they prepared their boys for the Selection? Get them to befriend someone, only to turn on them in the end?

"Why? Why did you do this, Phelan?" Eron said. His body convulsed as he sobbed. The movement hurt immensely, but it couldn't be stopped. He almost thought death would be a welcome escape from dealing with the realities he'd faced.

Why did Phelan turn on him like that? Was he really unworthy of living? Was he truly what Bello and Phelan said he was, a weak coward?

The soothing sounds of the flowing stream interrupted his train of thought. He welcomed the reprieve and let the sounds flow away with the current. Throbbing pain pulsated throughout his body.

When he awoke, Eron was completely disoriented. "Phelan," he said, "where are we?" Then he heard the rushing stream and all the events of the last days crashed over him. The pit inside grew larger still.

"How long was I out?" he said. No one answered. Standing was difficult, but he made it through the pain, though barely.

He thought he heard the snarl of craates. "Oh no," he said. He had no weapon, no strength, and hardly any will to fight left.

The snarl was cut off. Eron waited, but there was nothing.

A black figure scurried away from the direction of the sound. It didn't hide, standing in the open several meters away.

"The Forgotten," he said. He remembered it screaming at him to leave after saving him from Phelan.

Eron felt the pit inside grow again at the thought of Phelan.

Why is he following me?

For the moment, the Forgotten seemed content to leave him alone and he was grateful for that bit of luck.

"Kill me if you want! I don't have the strength to fight."

The Forgotten howled and raised an arm, pointing

towards the south and Victory Point. He wasn't sure if
he should be afraid or thankful for it.

Forty-Two

Eron travelled south through the woods along a barely visible path. Despite being beaten badly and his slow gait, he made decent time. Now and again, the Forgotten revealed himself, always pointing south. He didn't seem threatening any longer. Eron felt comforted by his presence, as though the Forgotten was a long-lost friend.

Eron's legs ached. He stopped, leaning on a tree. The Forgotten startled him.

"Why don't you go?" he said, making Eron jump and almost fall.

"Please, I mean no harm. I'm working my way south," Eron said, covering his head with his arms. The Forgotten was taller than him and covered in thick black hair.

"Why do you stay here? You must go. Soon you won't be able to leave. You'll be like me. You can be better."

The Forgotten's clear speech contrasted with his frightening presence. He should be afraid. But for some reason, the Forgotten didn't seem terrifying. It was as though he knew Eron.

"You have a day left. No more. After that, you will become like me. I don't want that for you," he said.

Eron tilted his head and squinted. "Why would you care what I become? Is it a territorial thing?" Whatever reservations Eron had about the Forgotten seemed wrong.

"You need to hurry. You have some distance to go, but must not be late. Being late is," he lowered his head, "bad. Don't be late."

As ferocious as the beast could be, his concern for Eron was unexpected and awkward, as if any moment the thing would snap and attack Eron, revealing his true nature.

Just like Phelan.

"Who are you? What is your name? Why do you care what happens to me?" Eron said.

The Forgotten reached out to a couple small trees nearby and shook them, howling. "I said keep going! Don't wait here long. There's only so much I can do for you!" He stared at Eron for a moment, then ran into the forest, leaving the boy completely confused.

"Why won't he attack me? He wants to talk? I need to get out of here before I lose the rest of my mind," Eron said aloud. He shook his head as if that would fix everything and proceeded south.

He didn't see the Forgotten for quite a while after, but he knew he was near. Eron heard growling and yelping in the distance, and then came across dead craates in his path, blood still oozing from their snouts.

Near sunset, he reached the edge of the forest and a powerful feeling of anxiety and relief came over him.

A plain of orange and red grass separated by a wide path spread out before him. At the far end of the plain stood a tall stone wall with a gate in the middle.

The end.

His final step along the Selection.

As he stepped out of the forest, the Forgotten raced up behind him. As Eron turned, his ribs and entire body rocked with pain. There was nothing he could do to defend himself from the Forgotten. It would be one last terrible fight. All the progress he'd made, all the terrible things he did to get to this point, only to be wiped away by the Forgotten.

It was the last betrayal he'd endure.

"What do you want?" Eron said. He held his hands out. His arms shook and he could barely stand straight.

The Forgotten pulled up short. "I'm not going to harm you. I wanted to say goodbye. This will be the last time we ever see each other."

Eron dropped his fists. "What are you talking about? Who are you? Why are you talking to me like this?"

"Eron," he said. Eron stepped back.

"How do you know my name? Did you hear the blue boy call me that?"

"Eron, you know me. Look inside you. You know who I am. I've been tracking you ever since you started your journey from Rippon. Do you remember we met in the valley? I've been watching you."

Eron stepped back again. "Stay away from me! Why are you doing this? All I want to do is get through that gate and be done with this forever."

"You will. You'll make it, Eron. Not like me. I couldn't. I wasn't strong enough. But you are. You did the right thing. You cared for others, Eron; you worked with strangers. Maybe that's what will change things. I don't know. I've been gone too long. But you're special, Eron; you aren't weak like I was. Or like Bello or the blue one. They were weak. Your strength-caring for others-carried you through all this."

Something about the Forgotten's voice sounded familiar. When he wasn't howling at Eron, he sounded so different.

"Timo?" Eron said, ashamed the moment he did. His brother died a long time ago.

The Forgotten closed his eyes and lowered his head. "I was once," he said. "It's not my name now. I'm too far gone. I'm part of the forest. That name was my old name from my old home. This is my home now. This is where I fight to survive every day."

Inside, Eron felt a flood of emotions overwhelm him. His brother was alive! He was here! He could leave with him!

"Timo! Come with me! We can go together!"

Timo howled. Eron raised his hands to his ears to block the frightening sound.

"I cannot leave, Eron. This is my place now. The Selection is wrong, Eron. You know it. Everything is wrong. But I can't do anything about it now. I did my part by making sure you lived. You can do something. You care for others. Your instinct isn't to kill; it's to care."

"I thought you were dead, Timo! For years, your screams have haunted me. Now, I find you alive? This is wonderful. Mom will want to know."

Timo raised a dark hairy paw.

"She will know nothing. You'll never be allowed to speak to her again. They're ruthless, Eron. They care only about covering their tracks and making sure you fall in line."

"What do you mean, I'll never talk to her again? I

don't understand."

"You must go, Eron. Time is running short for you. This is my place now, not yours. Be well, brother. You can change this. All of it."

Timo pointed towards the gate and stood for several minutes. Then he howled a fierce, piercing sound and ran back to the forest.

Suddenly Eron's memory returned. Rippon. Classes on Selection survival. The genetic mutation caused by a virus on the new planet, allowing male overpopulation. The other colonies, offshoots of the original. Everything he'd been fighting in his mind came back. It was as if Timo's presence tripped a switch that turned his thoughts back on. The haze which covered everything lifted and a clarity he hadn't known since Timo's disappearance returned.

"Timo, come back! Timo!" He started for the forest, ignoring the gate behind him. "Timo, please don't leave!"

Forty-Three

Eron considered running after his brother, but doing so would mean no Mina. No new life. No escape from the Selection. He watched as Timo ran away.

"Be well, brother. I will miss you," he said.

Eron marched toward the large stone gate of Victory Point and the end of his ordeal. Soldiers stood along the stone wall with their weapons drawn on him.

Was he too late? Were they going to shoot him? He shuffled faster, wanting to make it past the guns and through the gate before anything changed. The packed dirt crunched under his feet. When he came to the gate, he paused, taking a long look back the way he came. The forest looked serene, but he knew the horrors lurking within. Dead bodies of those he knew and trusted were back there. Bodies of boys who tried to harm him, in fact did harm him, lay back there. Never again would he have to face those terrors.

"Timo," he said in a quiet voice. "Goodbye."

Then he stepped through the gate to another world.

Beyond the gate, a carnival was in full swing. Red and white tents were scattered around the clearing. Music carried across the field. There were jugglers and acrobats. Barkers called others to their games. It was such a festive place, a stark contrast to what he'd just been through.

"Ah, another survivor!" said a man in a large, velvety red top hat. "Gentlemen, please give this one his due!"

A band struck up a song and the entire carnival stopped what they were doing and applauded Eron. Horns and drums and stringed instruments filled the air with a triumphant sound. The crowd cheered and whistled and patted him on the back, which hurt immensely.

The man with the top hat noticed his grimace and called for a medic. Soon a small medical team of all men dressed in white overalls hurried to Eron. They looked obscenely out of place in the middle of the carnival.

"Here, sit down," one of the medics said. Another medic unfolded a small canvas chair and pushed it towards him. Eron sat while the team looked him over from head to toe. They removed his shirt and bandaged his wounds. The lead medic cleaned his face and stared at the crooked nose. "This is gonna hurt. Hold on," he said. Taking Eron's nose in both hands, he set it back in place with a nasty pop. A sharp, blinding pain radiated from his nose. Eron screamed.

"You'll feel that for a little while, but it's fine. It might be a little crooked, but not too bad. I've seen worse come through here," he said to Eron. After the medical team cleaned and attended his major wounds, they scattered like insects in the light.

The man in the top hat cheered him on. "Huzzah! Great show! Now to find your mate! I mean, that is why you endured all this right?"

"Who are you?" Eron asked.

"Why, I'm the Ringleader! I run this at the request

of Her Majesty! Now I get to lead you to your ring. Well, to your lady waiting for a ring. Anyway, come this way, young man."

Eron hesitated. None of this made sense. Her Majesty? What was this guy talking about? There was no royalty in the colony. They were led by an elected council. Nobody ruled as a monarch. Those things were abolished on Earth and never carried to the colonies.

"Come on, Eron; this way, please. The ladies are waiting. We hoped for more of you, but it seems the Selection was extraordinarily difficult this go around. You're the last to arrive."

Eron couldn't help but notice the number of adult males in the celebration. He'd never seen so many older men in his life.

Maybe his father was here.

"Wait, how did you know my name? I never told you."

The man in the top hat grinned. It was an eerie look on the skinny man's face. "I'm the Ringleader. It's my job to know. Queen Anastasia the Greater, fifth of her name and ruler of this planet would not have it otherwise. Come now, don't be late." He giggled as he led Eron through the maze of tents and chaos.

"What queen? Anastasia? Isn't that our planet's name?" he said. A growing disorientation emerged inside. The Selection was difficult enough, but this was something completely new. And worrying. The Ringleader led him to a large gold and red tent in the center of the carnival. Armed male guards stood around it, their weapons in their arms.

"In here," the Ringleader said as he held open one

of the flaps.

Stepping inside, perfume and soft music overwhelmed him. It was a jarring contrast to the sounds and sights outside. In the center of the tent stood a riser with two rows of empty chairs. Soldiers removed all but three.

"One of those is for you," the Ringleader said. He escorted Eron to the side of the riser where two other boys stood waiting. One was blue-skinned like Phelan. At first, Eron thought it was his old friend and a mix of relief and anger flashed through him, but when he moved closer, he could see it was clearly not Phelan. The boys looked at him with beaming smiles.

"All right!" the blue boy said. "Now we get to start. Soon we'll get our brides and be off to a new life! I can't wait!"

Eron had no words for him.

The Ringleader left the three of them and stood against the far wall, watching the proceedings.

Forty-Four

Eron couldn't grasp what was happening. A few hours ago, he was having a conversation with what he thought was his dead brother. After being attacked by his one-time friend Phelan. After enduring a horrific, deadly journey through the forest, all for the sake of tradition.

Now, he stood inside a circus tent with two other boys that weren't trying to kill him and surrounded by mostly females of all ages and colors. If only Mina were here so he could start his new life with her, then all of this would be worth it.

The seated crowd hushed when a woman who looked to be a few years older than Eron stepped inside the tent, escorted by six armed soldiers. Behind her were three young women. He couldn't tell if one of them was Mina, but the last one in line resembled her.

The woman in the lead walked directly towards the boys and stopped in front of them.

"Congratulations, men, you made it through the Selection. Many enter and very few ever make it out alive. You are the last of this group. The rest were not as fortunate. The Selection is brutal, but it forces us to carry only the best to the next and future generations."

Eron stared at the woman. Her eyes were gold like Mina's. Her hair was straight and hung down to the middle of her back. She wore a crown of bright blue metal with a red stone in the center of her forehead.

"I salute you gentlemen for your accomplishment. Now please take a seat. You're almost done."

The boys sat in the chairs on the riser, Eron in the middle.

The woman stood in front of them and faced the crowd. Eron tried to see if any of the three girls that walked in with her was Mina. The guards stood in his way.

"I present to you the winners of the Selection!" she said, waving her hand to acknowledge the boys. The crowd erupted in applause. She held up her hand, silencing them. "These three are the champions of this Selection. They are the strongest, bravest, and smartest of them all. And now they get to be Chosen, as is the custom on our world. Ladies," she said to the three girls.

The soldiers parted and the three girls approached her. "Your Majesty," they said together, bowing.

"You have been selected to pair with the boys to continue humanity on Anastasia. Do you know your Chosen ones?"

"Yes, Queen Anastasia," they said in unison.

Queen? Queen Anastasia? What were they talking about? Eron thought.

There were two brown-haired girls and one reddish-haired girl. With curls. Eron strained to look, and there she was.

Mina!

She didn't look his way, but kept her attention on the queen. Then the girls turned to face the boys.

Eron's heart leapt at seeing Mina. Finally, after everything he'd endured, after all the physical and mental pain he went through, he was about to start his new life. The promise of the Selection had forced him to take on so much pain, and now, the payoff.

Mina!

The girl he'd been dreaming about since his time in the colony. The face that drove him forward when he wanted to give up. Soon, he would be free of the Selection and free to begin his life with her. He could barely contain his joy. A smile broke out on his cracked lips.

The girls approached the riser. Eron fidgeted in his seat. Mina looked at him and smiled. But there was something missing in her smile. It was...distant. Cold, even. Eron winced. What was wrong with her? Why did she act this way after all he went through to be here? Didn't she know how badly he wanted to be with her?

"Ladies, you may take your Chosen," the queen said. Eron started to stand and take Mina's hand, but she went to the blue boy instead.

"What?" Eron said.

One of the brown-haired girls approached Eron and grabbed his hand. "My Chosen, thank you for making it through the Selection. We will live a long life together," she said. She was beautiful, but Eron had no idea who she was.

"But Mina!" he said. "Why? I did all of this for you! I lived for you!"

"Silence!" the queen said. "You are paired according to biological compatibility. Before the Selection, you were paired with a certain young lady; surely you know this. You were selected for a specific purpose."

Selected? Predestined pairings? Yes! Yes, I do remember! It's not right. It's never been right.

Eron shuffled his feet.

Timo's voice rose in his head, reminding him he was the one to change it all. He had to do something about them, whoever they were. Eron thought he understood now. The queen. Her policies. The Selection.

It was all to cull unwanted genetics and pass on desirable traits, whatever those were. He understood how the humans on Anastasia were in danger.

Selected genetics, irrespective of human desire. They were forced into the illusion of a decision. They were forced to fight and kill each other. But only the boys. Something was wrong. The Selection was wrong.

If he was going to change it, he'd need to be calm. His brother said he was the one.

Right now, he believed him.

He looked to Mina, at the lovely face that encouraged him in the darkest moments. He knew now she'd never be his. She was never to be his in the first place. The pit inside him was gaping now, threatening to consume him.

Then a tug on his hand and he faced the young brown-haired girl in front of him. "I'm Sarai. Nice to meet you, Eron. We have a lot to talk about."

Eron looked past her at Mina. She walked out of the tent holding a blue hand in hers.

"Eron?" Sarai asked.

"Sorry, I was daydreaming. Hello, Sarai, let's get out of here." He held her hands in his and escorted her out of the tent as the gathered crowd parted ways and cheered.

Inside, Eron felt empty. Everything was wrong. He'd need to stay strong if he was going to make it right. Sarai would never know how he felt about Mina. Whatever this really was, he'd not give them the satisfaction of bringing him down with it.

Change wouldn't come easy. Patience in the face of absurdity would serve him well. "Sarai, let's get out of here. We've got much to discuss."

She smiled.

Inside himself, a deep hollow space as black as the night sky was illuminated by the tiniest light. He focused on the light, allowing it to glow and grow bigger. Anger turned to determination. Timo's words of encouragement comforted him, replacing the screams that once haunted him.

ACKNOWLEDGEMENTS

Thanks

Thank you so much for making it this far! It's been an amazing opportunity to share my world with you.

If you enjoyed *The Selection*, continue the story with the next book in the series, *Rise of the Forgotten*.

I'd like to thank my family for allowing me the time to pursue this dream. To my wife Jenny and son Jackson...thank you! It means everything to have you believe in me.

To my readers Aaron Hamilton and Johanna Haas, thank you for your kind suggestions and input. I hope the final version does your time justice.

To Kassidy Phoenix, thanks for your encouragement and investment in what I do. You rock!

To Sam Bell, thanks for your encouragement over the years. It's meant so much.

To my editor Jodi McDermitt and original cover artist Dan Brown, thanks a bunch for making me look better than what I am.

My fellow writers who've encouraged me and offered

sage advice, I thank you: Aaron Hamilton, Thomas Gunther, Brent Harris, Stephen Hunt, Maria Haskins, John Smith, Ray Wenck, and many many more. You guys are the best!

And finally dear reader, thank you for allowing me to entertain you. I hope that you'll take a moment and leave a review. Your voice helps others discover my work. Without you, I wouldn't have the opportunity to share my stories.

Thank you, thank you, thank you!

ABOUT THE AUTHOR

Jason J. Nugent has been a paperboy, pizza maker, dishwasher, restaurant manager, promotional products sales rep, chamber of commerce director, and one time BBQ champion. He has skated with Tony Hawk, had a babysitter with a serial killer brother, and is followed by rapper Chuck D on Twitter. He and his wife share a home in beautiful Southern Illinois with their son, two cats, and two dogs.

He's the author of the thrilling young adult scifi series *The Forgotten Chronicles: The Selection, Rise of the Forgotten, The War for Truth* and two collections of horror / dark fiction short stories: *(Almost) Average Anthology* and *Moments of Darkness*.

More information and his blog can be found at jasonjnugent.com.